Magic Can't Save Us

Eighteen Tales of Likely Failure

T0414090

Magic Can't Save Us

Eighteen Tales of Likely Failure

Josh Denslow

University of New Orleans Press

ISBN: 9781608012718

First edition
Printed in the United States of America on acid-free paper.

University of New Orleans Press
2000 Lakeshore Drive
New Orleans, Louisiana 70148

unopress.org

Cover design by Kevin Stone

Library of Congress Cataloging-in-Publication Data

Names: Denslow, Josh author
Title: Magic can't save us : 18 tales of likely failure / Josh Denslow.
Other titles: Magic cannot save us
Description: New Orleans : UNO Press, 2025.
Identifiers: LCCN 2025002171 (print) | LCCN 2025002172 (ebook) | ISBN 9781608012718 paperback | ISBN 9781608012756 epub | ISBN 9781608012763 pdf
Subjects: LCSH: Interpersonal relations--Fiction | LCGFT: Fantasy fiction | Short stories
Classification: LCC PS3604.E5875 M34 2025 (print) | LCC PS3604.E5875 (ebook) | DDC 813/.6--dc23/eng/20250310
LC record available at https://lccn.loc.gov/2025002171
LC ebook record available at https://lccn.loc.gov/2025002172

For Rebecca, who loved these stories before I did.

Part 1:
Beginnings are Fraught

Part 2:
The Middle Reveals Problems

Part 3:
No Such Thing as Second Chances

Part 4:
The End is Nigh

Part 5:
The End

"As you can see, I have absolutely no sense of humour," he said.

— Olga Tokarczuk,
Drive Your Plow Over the Bones of the Dead

Part 1:
Beginnings Are Fraught

Tale #1: Keening

I'm in a wild mood tonight. I want to go dance in the foam.
I hear the banshees calling.

— Raymond Chandler, *Farewell, My Lovely*

I have my own personal banshee. Most mornings, usually
during my second bowl of cereal, she lets out a soul-melting
wail to give me a heads-up on my impending death. I used to
get worried, but it's been a while. And I'm still here.

Most people don't notice her right away. She has long
gray hair that falls in clumps across her face, but her traveling cloak, which pools around her feet and has a voluminous
hood, tends to match the colors of whatever room she's in,
which is always the room I'm in. She's forever there with me.
In every space I occupy.

She only wails in the morning though. Like she is right now.

"What's it going to be this time?" I say. "Chicken bone? E.
coli? Trampoline accident?" I dunk my spoon into my milk,
foraging for marshmallows.

"Mock me at your peril," she whispers in a voice that
grinds bones.

"Fuck, dude," my roommate says from the front room.
"I didn't know she talked too. That should have been in the
lease. It's unnerving. She sounds like she has pleurisy."

1

My roommate has been reading a lot of Charles Dickens and has a bunch of new words he's been trying out. But what he says is true. I haven't heard my banshee talk in months. Maybe even years.

I glance in her direction, but her intensity causes me to look down at my cereal again.

"Today is the day," my banshee says in barely a whisper. My roommate doesn't hear.

"I really hope not," I say. For once, some of her gloom has managed to permeate my mood. "I have a date tonight."

My banshee has been with me since I was ten, when I fell onto the subway tracks trying to reach someone's abandoned Happy Meal toy. My mom wouldn't take me to McDonald's so I really coveted those cheap, plastic movie tie-in figures with non-articulated limbs and personified chicken nuggets with terrified looks on their faces. I remember the cement rushing up at me. The rank smell of wet sludge soaking my shirt. The vibration of the coming train.

And then the keening. A sound that at the time, I had no name for. A plaintive wail that pierced my eardrums at such a high decibel that I stopped trying to find a way out and instead covered my ears with my bleeding hands.

My banshee was looking down from the platform, her nostrils flared, one notched finger pointing at me. Then some guy jumped onto the track and threw me back onto the platform. He barely got out himself before the train rumbled into the station.

"I heard that horrific sound, and I knew something was wrong," the guy said, unable to look at the woman in the cloak who had sounded the alarm.

My banshee accidentally saved me, and since that moment, she hasn't let me out of her sight.

At the time, as our relationships with friends and family began to crumble due to a harbinger of death following me everywhere, my mom thought perhaps I needed to do more to shake the banshee. She tracked down the guy who had pulled me from the tracks, convinced I needed to thank him.

Unfortunately, he'd died of a heart attack a few days after saving me. After that, my mom began finding millions of reasons to never be home.

#

After my banshee's morning proclamation, I try to ignore her amplified intensity because I'm already a bit nervous about my date tonight with my roommate's sister.

A couple of months ago, his sister stopped by to say goodbye before she moved across the country. But then something truly strange happened. Not only was she not scared of my banshee, she was intrigued by her. She tried to engage her in conversation. She touched her cloak. Complimented her hair. I'd never seen anything like it. I felt immediately drawn to my roommate's sister. She was like one of those McDonald's Happy Meal Toys. Something I didn't think I could ever have in my life.

When I heard she was returning for a visit, I asked my roommate if I could arrange some time to see her. And that time was on the schedule for tonight. At a restaurant.

But my banshee seems eager to ruin my excitement. As I dress for work, she exhales a series of painful-sounding, ragged breaths that make it difficult for me to button my shirt properly on the first try. She has her crooked back tucked into the corner, her pale hands splayed on the wall. I'm scared to look away from her to tie my shoes.

I've spent a huge portion of my life with my banshee, but we rarely interact. This full-frontal pivot into my daily activities breaks an unspoken agreement we've maintained for years.

I get up to leave, and my banshee darts into the front room ahead of me. When I catch up, my roommate is staring at her in horror. "I can't imagine why my sister is interested in something so sepulchral," he says.

"She's interested in my banshee because she has a kind heart," I say.

"Our whole life she was always taking in dogs with three legs or cats with one eye or birds with broken wings. And always full of sassigassity."

"That's a Dickens word?" I ask.

"Yes, he made that one up."

"Sounds like it."

"Anyway, the point is. You're the only one calling it a date."

Then he opens his copy of *Bleak House* and continues reading.

#

Sometimes even I can't find my banshee once we step outside. She blends into crowds so well, it borders on invisibility. But I feel her with me always. Today, though, it's more intense. A palpable connection between us. Unlike most days when I walk to work, when I can pretend for a brief time that I don't have a banshee at all, I keep catching sight of her. Up a tree. On a roof. Whizzing between two cars. There's a prickle on my neck. A cold sweat on my back. I know there wasn't anything different about my banshee's warning today, but suddenly the world feels full of obstacles. Parallel universes of possible deaths.

I slow my pace. I try not to establish eye contact. I proceed to work.

My apartment is only six blocks from the advertising agency where I spend my days. I used to share an office with a recent college graduate who'd started as an intern and moved up quickly in the ranks. But a freak bike accident a few months ago removed her from the mortal realm, and now I have my own office.

I get immediately to work writing copy for a popular brand of toilet paper, and then suddenly, my banshee is humming. It's a slow dirge, something apocalyptic in its note choices, and I quickly jot down *Believe the hype, this is the world's best wipe* before I forget it.

4

"What exactly are you doing?" I ask my banshee, who is crouched so perfectly in a shadow near the door that three people have come in to talk to me this morning and no one noticed her.

"You like?" she whispers, her voice like ten thousand fingernails on ten thousand chalkboards.

"Not even a little," I say.

"Too bad." Then she starts humming again.

#

My boss hates my idea for the toilet paper. So I wrap up early, eager to move to the portion of the night where I see my roommate's sister. The humming has thankfully stopped, but my banshee seems to be standing out more. She stays right next to me so I can't get even one moment of relief.

I'm pretty sure my old boss would have loved my toilet paper idea. I've seen a million toilet paper ads, and I've never seen one rhyme *hype* and *wipe*. My old boss was more willing to take chances, but he was really unnerved by my banshee.

"Can't she stay at home?" he asked once.

"You try to tell her," I said.

But he never got the chance, because he was involved in a fatal car accident the very next weekend.

#

I stop at the apartment to shower quickly and change before my date with my roommate's sister. My roommate is still on the couch, but now he has his computer and his sheafs of paper and his coffee thermos and his bag of jelly beans. This is the visual clue that he's doing his work as a book editor and not just reading Dickens.

My banshee clambers up the wall behind him as I try to slip past without interrupting.

"I can tell from here that you still think this is a date tonight," my roommate says.

"I'm sorry," I say. "I can't help it. I'm intrigued by your sister. Quite a bit."

My roommate nods. "Fair enough. She is pretty cool." Then he sees my banshee on the wall behind him, peering down like some kind of decrepit falcon. He jumps to his feet and stumbles across the room away from her.

"What the deuce!" he cries. "You could have told me she was right behind me."

"I'm sorry," I say. "She has me rattled today too."

My roommate looks at me. "I was thinking earlier. How do you know when she screams every morning that it's not for someone else? A banshee predicts deaths. Maybe someone dies when you don't, man. You ever think about that?"

"People die every day," I say. "I think it's like every minute or something. I could start keening every morning and claim to know someone would die that day. And I'd be right. Someone is definitely going to die. But I think it's different with my banshee. It's some kind of penance for getting it wrong back when I was ten. Like she sees me every day and remembers, oh yeah, this guy is supposed to be dead. Maybe she's hoping each day it will finally happen and she'll be free."

My banshee stares at me, her lips pursed.

"How do you know that's how it works?" my roommate asks.

Air whistles through my banshee's flared nose.

"I just know." I wish he would move to another topic. My lack of understanding is making me uncomfortable, especially under the piercing stare of my banshee.

"It's for me," I say. "I promise." I don't tell him how my previous roommate had similar concerns. Before moving out, he became convinced she was keening for him. But he didn't actually die until after he'd moved into his new apartment across town. So obviously there was no connection. But, either way, I never include any of that in the apartment listing.

"I better get in the shower," I say. "I don't want to be late."

My banshee leaps from her perch on the wall and follows me more closely than usual. Her breath tickles the small hairs on my neck.

"Say your vespers," my roommate says as I walk into the bathroom.

My banshee sits on the counter while I shower, and the steam loosens a few of the knots in her hair. She looks sad, her face slightly distorted through the clear curtain, beads of water running down the plastic like tears. She's made it impossible over the years to have meaningful relationships and maintain long-term friendships, and she's completely ruined masturbating, but I feel this little pang of remorse. As if there is something I need to apologize for.

She shifts back to the corner behind the toilet while I towel-dry and get dressed. When I return to the front room, my roommate is on his feet, anticipating my exit.

"Couple of things about my sister."

"I won't let anything happen to her."

My roommate nods like he believes it. "She hates when guys tell her she's pretty. And she hates when guys try to pay for her meal."

"Are you setting me up?"

"Why would I set you up?"

"So I bomb with your sister."

His face doesn't change. "I think you can handle that part yourself."

At that moment, my banshee begins to hum again.

"Ah humbug. That shit is scary. Get out of here before I call my sister and tell her not to meet you."

I move quickly to the door.

"And whatever you do, please, please, please don't let my sister adopt her."

#

When I arrive at the restaurant, my banshee hurries ahead and settles behind a plant before I'm through the door.

"I'm meeting someone," I say to the hostess, and I get this little thrill in my chest.

"I think she's here already," she says as she grabs a menu. The thrill in my chest turns into an explosion.

My roommate's sister looks exactly as I remember her. There's something really pleasing about that. And she seems happy. She's pulsing with energy, like a downed power line snapping and popping on cement.

"Hi," I say.

She looks up and appraises me. There's a twinkle, like she's about to tell a joke. "Hi," she says and returns to browsing the menu. "A lot of stuff sounds good here."

"Yes," I say.

"You planning on using only one syllable words?"

"No," I say, and then we both laugh.

"At least sit down. You're freaking me out."

I sit down as she looks over the menu at me.

"Panoply," I say.

"Pardon me?"

"Sorry. That was the first multi-syllable word that came to mind," I say.

"Why?"

"I write copy for ads. My boss didn't like my idea today, and he told me to think of the product as a panoply."

"A panoply of what?"

"Toilet paper," I say.

She thinks for a second, her eyes half-closing in a way that feels like I'm being shown a secret. "Any way to have it be a play on words? Panoply. Ply. Three-ply toilet paper."

There's no going back now. Ever. "That's genius," I say.

She laughs and returns to her menu. "Pick something to eat so we can skip the part where the waitress comes and neither of us know what we want and we're doomed to repeat this section of the meal again."

"Okay," I say, but I don't look at the menu. "Your brother told me not to say you're pretty and not to try to pay for your meal."

"It's true. Impressive. He must like you."

"Am I allowed to think it?"

"No," she says.

I don't really want to look away from her, so I quickly scan the menu and choose the first thing I see. When I look up, my roommate's sister has her menu down too.

"So. Where is she? Did she not come?"

"Who?" I ask. But I know.

She looks around the room. There's no way she'll find her without my help.

I sigh and point to the plant near the kitchen. "She's over there, but she's been off today. Upset about something."

My roommate's sister gasps.

Something sinks deep inside me. I'd thought she was going to be okay with my banshee. "I know she can be a bit much to take in."

"Oh, she doesn't bother me," she says. "I was just shocked she's hiding behind a plant."

She gets up and walks directly toward my banshee. My banshee shrinks away from her, but she doesn't run.

"Remember me?" my roommate's sister says.

My banshee nods brusquely.

"You don't have to sit here. Why don't you join us?"

My banshee doesn't respond. My heart slams blood through my veins at triple speed.

"No pressure," my roommate's sister says. "You're welcome at any time." She returns, grabbing an empty chair along the way, and places it along the side of the table between us. Then she sits down again.

"Let's order," she says, waving for a waitress who honestly looks pretty terrified of my banshee. "Do you know what your banshee likes?"

"I mean," I say. "I don't think I've ever seen her eat."

"She has to eat. Take a guess. What do you think she would like?"

I look at the menu. "Spaghetti?"

"No," my banshee says, suddenly in her seat, her voice plunging into my ear like a stake.

"Pick anything you want," my roommate's sister says.

"Stuffed mushrooms," my banshee intones.

"I like those too," my roommate's sister says and then turns back to me. "You know you wince every time she talks?"

"I don't think so. Not every time."

"You do," my banshee says and holds out the final syllable until all the air has been released from her lungs.

My roommate's sister shakes her head at me. "Do you two ever talk?"

And it is as if my banshee and I were on a sitcom. We looked at each other like that was the craziest thing we'd ever heard. All that was missing was a laugh track.

"If you two talked," my roommate's sister says, "you could suggest things, like, 'Maybe you could wait in the other room while I change or use the bathroom,' or whatever. You could pick up her favorite food for her on your way home from work. There's no reason you have to spend every waking moment together."

"I'm not the one who sets the rules," I say.

My banshee stares at me. "There are no rules."

I have always been under the impression we have all these unspoken rules. That there has been some logical, even metaphysical, steering of the situation that we are living through. I suddenly can't breathe. My head feels too light on my neck.

"You spend all your time ignoring her. Pretending like she isn't there. She wants you to see her. She literally screams every morning to get your attention."

My banshee opens her mouth, her jaw hinging audibly. Dust falls from the wrinkles in her face and sputters on the table.

"I've watched you grow up," she says, the words like whips

on an exposed back. "I've watched you become a man."

It was true. She watched me sprout hair in awkward places and make the same mistakes multiple times before learning anything. She saw all the times I doubted myself and talked myself out of doing the right thing in difficult situations. She knew how much the world frightened me.

"See?" my roommate's sister says. "Isn't it beautiful?"

Now they are both staring at me. I no longer have any grasp on what constitutes beautiful. But I know for sure I've made a horrible mistake. And I've been making the same mistake over and over for years. Instead of unspoken rules, we could have had real rules. We could have worked together. She was with me through everything. Watching. Warning. The only constant, really. My dad had bailed before my subway accident, and my mom was too focused on herself. I was left to make a life of my own.

My roommate was totally right. This didn't feel like a date at all.

But then the waitress is standing here. She will not look at my banshee, and I feel a wave of anger wash over me. Why won't she look at her? She's sitting right here at the table with us.

My roommate's sister closes her menu and gets up. "I'm in the way. I think you two should have this dinner together. Talk it out. Then call me."

"I want to see you again," I say in a panic.

"It's possible," she says and pats me on the head. "My brother does seem to like you." She turns to my banshee. "Nice to see you again."

"You too," my banshee says like gravel caught in a lawnmower, and this time I see my roommate's sister wince. Just a little.

"Do you still want to eat?" the waitress asks.

"We'll both have the stuffed mushrooms," I say, and she nearly trips as she runs from our table back to the kitchen.

But my banshee doesn't care whether our waitress is rude or not. She's watching my roommate's sister walk across the restaurant. She opens the door and lets a burst of traffic and human noise into the room. As much as I want her to, she doesn't look back.

Then my banshee jumps to her feet, her cloak shivering like melting ice, and begins keening at a pitch I've never heard. The other people in the restaurant fall from their chairs, clutching their ears.

But unlike the other times I've heard her plaintive wail, I look directly at her. Then I follow her eyes through the front window and onto the sidewalk, where my roommate's sister waits to cross the street.

The keening gets even louder.

I spring from the table, leaping over people curled in fetal positions on the floor, and run after her as if all our lives depend on it.

Tale #2: Bingo

This is the way the world ends; not with a bang
or a whimper, but with zombies breaking down
the back door.

— Amanda Hocking, *Hollowland*

A stranger and I sit in adjacent booths in a coffee shop, and when the internet crashes, we look up from our dating apps like groundhogs discovering our shadows. She lifts her delicate hand, her finger arched like a stamen, and pushes an imaginary button between us.

"Bingo," she says.

Behind me, two people jump up from their table so quickly that silverware clatters to the floor along with the dregs of their coffee. They push against each other, elbows and shoulders shuffling, in a frantic rush to leave.

I know I should join them, but when I turn around, the stranger now sits across from me.

"I'm Lily," she says.

In all the commotion, I didn't see her move. She has a face so beautiful it seems almost impossible for her to exist. After the way things ended with my ex, it's easy to feel like I'll never be able to hold onto that kind of beauty again.

"You Bingo'd me," I say, somewhat dumbfounded.

She shrugs. "Tell me one thing that isn't on your Bingo profile."

"I'm not as funny as I think I am," I say.

"No one is."

"I guess I'm pretty lonely."

"The human condition."

I suddenly want to tell her something she can't render mundane. "I got a boner once when I was petting a cat."

She laughs so hard that her dark eyes narrow and her nose wrinkles, and I want to be the only person in the world to ever cause that to happen again. And maybe I am. Maybe today will be our last day ever.

"Will you marry me?" I ask.

"Let's start smaller," she says.

"How about a scone?"

"Deal."

I go to the counter, but all the employees have walked away. The coffee machine gurgles and the refrigerator whirrs. Then they both stop at the same time. The electricity has gone out.

I turn and watch the ceiling fan above Lily slowly come to a rest. The last remaining small group begins stuffing croissants and bagels into their bags and then pushes out into the street. A siren wails somewhere across town.

Lily and I are alone.

"Everyone's gone," I say. A dozen people run past the front window, car horns blaring at them. "Should we go?"

Lily glances around the empty coffee shop. "I want to finish my coffee first. I'm tired of running away."

I return to my chair. "They always want us to run," I say. "And it's really hard because they don't provide lids for our cups here."

She laughs again, but this one is different. It's a defense mechanism. "Here's something I don't write on my profile," she says. "I'm uncomfortable outside the noise of the world. If

I'm seen in any way, I slip away."

And in that moment, I feel I can truly see her.

"If it makes you feel any better, no one ever notices me," I say.

She nods. "Not until all the distractions are gone. And then, there you are. Across the coffee shop."

We lapse into a perfect silence where we drink coffee and spiritually lean into each other. The coffee shop is so quiet now that I can hear my nervous system buzzing in my ears.

Then someone bangs against the front window as they run by, and the sounds of the world come rolling back. People yelling. Tires crunching on glass. Metal on metal. And all the sirens, like surround sound, converging on us.

"Why did your last girlfriend leave you?" Lily asks.

"Who said she left me?"

"You did. When you said you were lonely and you weren't funny. Like you'd been spending a lot of time wondering what went wrong."

I can't argue. "Actually, my ex left me because she said I didn't fight for her. Which I didn't. But I would've also had to fight this really huge guy from her work."

"You have to choose your battles."

"A battle is only a battle if you want to win."

A door creaks open somewhere in the kitchen. Something heavy drags along the floor. Lily doesn't seem to notice. In any other scenario, I would have left by now. I would have been running with the rest of the city, lost in a crowd, alone. Soon everyone would be underground. But here in this coffee shop, I was blissfully in the open. I was taking up space. I was seen.

"I haven't given a Bingo to anyone in the app for weeks," she says. "But I keep scrolling and scrolling and scrolling. And I never look up."

"I Bingo everyone," I say.

She shakes her head with a smile. "Sounds pathetic."

"Didn't I mention that? I'm pathetic too. In addition to

my other great qualities."

We lock eyes as she takes her last sip of coffee. "Yes," she says.

"What?"

"I'll marry you."

"I don't think I was kidding," I say.

Her eyes close, and her lips part enough for me to catch a glimpse of her top teeth. "I don't think I am either. Life is a risk, and I stopped taking risks for some reason."

Then someone rams into my back and I lunge forward, my coffee spilling across the table. A guy moves toward Lily in a shirt that says LIFE IS A BEACH across the back.

The guy staggers and then falls onto her lap. She tries to push him away, but he clutches her around the waist. I grab a fistful of his hair and it peels off, scalp and all, and ends up as a clump of goo in my hand.

The man lifts himself until he and Lily are face to face. He takes hold of the back of her chair with both hands.

"That's my fiancée!" I yell. It feels good to say it.

The man gurgles a wet, inhuman sound, and Lily punches him in the forehead.

That's when it becomes clear that we waited too long. We should have left when the internet cut out. Somehow the zombies have breached the perimeter again, and we just missed the entire lockdown procedure. But I know we haven't made a mistake. If we'd left right away, we wouldn't be together. We would have fled as strangers. So here I am with the most interesting girl I've ever met, probably will ever meet, and she is about to be eaten right in front of me. And then I'll be next.

I leap forward and grab the zombie's shoulders. His flesh bunches in my hands like slices of bologna, but I hold tight as Lily pushes against his chest with her feet. He has an iron grip on the back of her chair, his mouth spitting and spraying as he snaps at her face. I widen my stance and yank, but even combined with the pressure Lily is exerting, we are all locked in this position.

I look over the zombie's shoulder. There is Lily looking back at me.

"Bingo!" she yells.

"Bingo!" I yell back.

I have chosen my battle.

Tale #3: Infinite Possibilities Outside the Screen

"That is too bad, because lack of communication with horses has impeded human progress," said Abrenuncio. "If we ever broke down the barriers, we could produce the centaur."

— Gabriel García Márquez, *Of Love and Other Demons*

My girlfriend has a new coworker, and she suddenly has a lot more meetings. I've passed by while her new coworker's head filled her computer monitor, and I don't blame her for wanting to look. He's an incredible testament to the astonishing aesthetic heights the human face can achieve. In the meantime, I just look like me.

"Your new coworker has set a new beauty benchmark," I say as we eat sushi I picked up from her favorite restaurant. We're on the couch with matching plates propped on our laps and our two cats sit in between us.

"I guess," my girlfriend says. "A couple of people in the office think he might be a centaur."

"Is that possible?" I say, because what else can I say after a statement like that.

"Well only if the bottom half of his body is a horse." She uses chopsticks for her sushi, and I use a fork. She delicately lifts a piece of tuna, and my heart is eradicated. I want to ask her to marry me, but I'm not a centaur. Never will be.

"No one has ever seen him in person," my girlfriend continues.

"Stands to reason then."

"What do you mean?" she says, and I hear this little annoyance in her voice that I've never noticed before.

"Well that he can be anything," I say. "There are infinite possibilities of what's going on outside his camera view until someone sees him. He could also have the body of a koala bear or an egret."

"Those aren't real things," she says and goes back to her sushi, the conversation over.

I cut into a California roll, and it falls apart.

#

The next morning while my girlfriend spends longer than her usual amount of time getting ready for a meeting, I go online to search if centaurs are real. I don't purport to know everything in this world, and who am I to shut down the possibility of a man with a horse body? Not like the way my girlfriend shut down my koala bear and egret suggestions.

I discover a raging debate on message boards where a lot of seemingly lonely people insist that centaurs exist while a lot of other seemingly lonely people insist that they don't. The one thing they all appear to agree on is that real or not, a centaur would be sweet and courteous and what can only be described as horrifically well-endowed.

My girlfriend's computer dings across the room. I close my centaur research and clear my search history. My girlfriend doesn't seem to have heard her computer. The bathroom door remains closed, mysterious clinking sounds reverberating on the other side.

I cross to her computer and feel a pressure in my chest. I'm doing something I know is wrong. I shouldn't look. But I want to look. I've never once invaded her privacy. But what if this is the moment where I could skip future heartbreak? Like here I am hoping to marry her one day, but maybe she's already moving on. While this debate rages in my head, I sit down and move the mouse to turn on the monitor.

And there it is. A message from Bradley Hoof: *You ready?*

Why did his last name have to be Hoof? And ready for what?

In my heightened, privacy-invasion mode, I sense a shift behind the bathroom door. I quickly put my girlfriend's computer to sleep and walk into the kitchen to eat three bowls of cereal and think about Bradley Hoof.

My girlfriend looks so beautiful when she emerges from the bathroom that I feel an excited shift in my boxers. She walks right past me and turns her computer monitor away from me so I can no longer see it. And she puts on headphones.

Distraught, I enter the bathroom, the air still swirling with the aromas of my girlfriend's lotions and sprays. I pull out my penis and take a good, hard look at it. I find it overwhelmingly underwhelming. I try to see it as my girlfriend would see it, like from the point of view of whether she'd be okay only seeing my penis forever. It looks so small and disappointing in the bathroom lighting that I decide not to let her see me naked for the foreseeable future.

#

When Bradley Hoof leaves the house after spending the day talking to my girlfriend on the internet, he has perfect posture and a pressed shirt. And he trots. His hooves sing on the pavement. *You ready?* he says to every woman he passes.

Or at least, I assume so.

#

I'm currently in between jobs. But my grandfather died last

year and left me some money, and now my main goal in life is to make this lack-of-job thing official. Most afternoons I pretend to go to the local coffee shop and fill out job applications, but really, I go to the movies. If you want to watch a movie every day, you will very quickly run out of options. Many days, I will watch something for the second or third time, and there's something strangely gratifying about it. I feel safe enveloped by scenes in which I know every outcome. I know what everyone is going to say and the consequence of every action. There are no surprises. It's like the movie is embracing me and cooing to me and telling me that everything is going to turn out fine.

Today, though, after invading my girlfriend's privacy, I can't stop thinking about Bradley Hoof. I don't want to watch a movie; I want to prove my girlfriend wrong. I want to track down her new coworker and show her that he is not a centaur. He can't offer her anything more than what I'm offering her. Then I can finally ask her to marry me.

I wish I'd seen this exact movie before and already knew how it ended.

So for once, I actually go to the coffee shop, and I pull out my laptop and start searching for Bradley Hoof.

I find five of them in my town. Knowing there are five people named Bradley Hoof drains even more of my virility. What if they all look like him? What if they are all centaurs?

I decide not to contemplate what that would do to my psyche and instead gather addresses.

The first is only a few blocks away. When I arrive at his building, I walk right up to his door. I feel pretty bold. I knock before I can talk myself out of it.

A short, balding guy answers.

"Are you Bradley Hoof?" I ask.

"Yes," he says.

"No, you're not," I say and walk away.

#

I pick up our favorite sushi again and return home to find my girlfriend hunched over a notebook at the kitchen table. A strand of her hair has come loose and waves across her forehead like a pendulum. As if letting me know time is running out to man up and move us along to the next phase in our relationship. But the Bradley Hoof impedance must be overcome first.

"You're staring at me while holding raw fish?" my girlfriend says.

"I suppose I am."

She closes her notebook and looks at me. "I love that sushi place, but we're at five days in a row now. Have you been cheating on me or something?"

This weird half-laugh and half-choke sound comes out of my mouth. I almost drop the sushi.

"I was just kidding," she says and takes the bag from me. She puts her hand on my shoulder for a brief moment as she passes, and it reminds me how little intimacy we've had in the last few weeks. I need to stop staring at my penis after she goes to bed and instead try to put it to use. We can always turn out the lights.

"Last day of sushi," I say and grab our plates before sitting next to her on the couch. Both of our cats appear as if from some alternate dimension and sit in the space between us. I'm not a huge fan of cats, but I have never once said those words out loud. Instead, I let their fur collect on my clothes and sometimes, inexplicably, in a very annoying way around my nose and under my eyes. Then I have to try to remove it by using my hand, like one of those skill cranes at the supermarket checkout where children try to extract toys from a bin.

"How is everything at work going?" I ask after taking my first bite.

"Fine. I've had so many meetings lately. My eyes are aching."

I know I shouldn't ask, but I do it anyway. "Why did you turn your monitor away."

She sighs. "Truthfully, I found it kind of weird the way you were talking about my new coworker. You seemed fixated on him."

In an expert move, my girlfriend has turned it around on me. It isn't that she is hiding anything, it's that I have been weird about him. The only thing I can do is apologize and assure her I didn't mean anything by it—that there is no way I would find out his name and try to track down where he lives to confront him. That's what a crazy person would do.

"Oh, sorry," I say. "I don't even remember what he looks like now. I was probably just trying to make you laugh."

#

Before Bradley Hoof returns home after an evening of equine debauchery, he trots silently to the street in front of our apartment and looks up at our bedroom window. The wind lightly tousles his perfectly coifed hair, and his animal magnetism wakes my girlfriend from a deep slumber. The window is strangely lit, like she's in that Dracula movie that Francis Ford Coppola directed. I'm prone in the bed, unable to move to stop her.

Or at least, this feels very possible. Or likely?

#

The next day, I leave before my girlfriend starts work. We did not have sex last night like I had planned because I'd become terrified that I wouldn't be able to sustain an erection. Instead of going to the movies or to the coffee shop, I go directly to the second address on my Bradley Hoof list. I end up having to take two buses, and it takes up most of my morning. I stare out the window the whole time, wondering if I'll catch sight of a centaur out there amongst the regular, bipedal people going about their day. It is better than thinking about my girlfriend being in a meeting with Bradley Hoof.

When I arrive at the duplex, I know immediately it isn't the right one. I feel inside that my Bradley Hoof doesn't live here. I ring the bell with barely any trepidation and wait. Finally a meek man shuffles to the door, his skin nearly translucent. I almost laugh.

"Bradley Hoof?" I say.

He nods the way a meek man with translucent skin would if he was scared to find a stranger at his door.

"Most definitely, you are not," I say. "Not even close."

#

By modifying my return route slightly, I am able to pass by the third option, and the moment I see it, I realize why the other two didn't feel right. This one is a low-slung house in a more residential part of town. But the gate out front has a wide arch, and there are double doors leading into the house that both swing open, almost like a barn. Like a horse could walk in.

I leave immediately in terror.

#

On the way home, I can't stop myself. I buy more sushi. My girlfriend looks displeased when I arrive, which of course isn't exactly what I'm going for.

"I got different rolls," I say.

She closes her computer and takes the bag from me, but this time she doesn't touch my arm. My skin prickles in the spot where we connected yesterday. As if my hair follicles are calling out to her.

I get the plates and we sit in our normal spots, and the cats appear. I know everything about this is wrong.

"The problem is, you don't know what my second favorite restaurant is," my girlfriend says finally. "You feel bad about not having a job, and you're attempting grand romantic gestures, but you stall out at picking up sushi and using the word sex when you aren't talking about filling out a government form."

"What is your second-favorite restaurant?"

"I don't know. I don't actually catalog things that way. I'm just saying. You don't know it. You *should* know it, not me." She pops a piece of sushi into her mouth. "But I love this new roll you got. So good. Also, if you want to fuck my brains out later, I have some availability."

I nod, even as my disappointing penis sends me messages that he can't possibly reach her brains.

#

The next day, I leave early again to eliminate the last two Bradley Hoofs. The first one lives in a massive apartment building on the seventeenth floor, and there is no way a centaur could fit in the elevator or the stairwell. But I have to be sure.

When he answers the door at the end of a dim hallway, he's just a regular guy. Nondescript. Not worthy of his name.

"Someone told me you were Bradley Hoof," I say.

"Correct," he says.

"You wish." I turn to leave quickly. Then I realize the hallway is long, and now this guy is watching me as I walk as fast as I can to hit the elevator call button.

"What exactly are you getting out of this exchange?" the man calls down the hallway as I try to wait for the elevator more casually than I have ever waited for an elevator in my life.

I figure I'm never going to see this guy again. "I'm trying to feel better about myself."

"Did it work?"

"Yes. I think it did. A little."

"At my expense?"

"Of course. It had to be you."

The man ponders that for a moment and then goes back into his apartment and shuts the door. I think that means I won. Then the elevator never shows up, and I have to walk down seventeen flights of stairs to leave.

#

Denying the reality of Bradley Hoofs has become a sort of hobby, and I find myself wishing there were more of them in my town as I approach the home of the last one. A town-home with a door too small for a centaur. I knock loudly, somewhat emboldened after my experience in the apartment building. In the end, it was invigorating to walk down all those stairs.

A man with long hair answers, a beard threatening to take over his face. "Hey, man. Do I know you?"

"No," I say. "But are you Bradley Hoof?"

The man squints at me and leans forward. "You may never know the answer to that."

"It's a simple question," I say, desperate to get to my favorite part.

"You think so, but really you're talking to yourself. You want to know. Are YOU Bradley Hoof." The man sizes me up. "And I can tell you, you don't have what it takes to be Bradley Hoof. You lack the fortitude. You lack the insight. You lack the power. Man, you couldn't be less Bradley Hoof if you tried."

Other than the complete burning sensation I feel, I am also a little in awe. He is so much better at this than I am. My throat makes a dry, clicking sound.

"Have a good day," he says, laughing a little. And then he's gone.

#

I'm in no shape to return to the barn door house that most likely contains the Bradley Hoof I'm looking for. I go home without sushi. Without a second-place restaurant. Just my empty hands and my broken heart. Because if anyone knows that I'm not Bradley Hoof, it's my girlfriend.

As I put the key in the lock, I hear her laughing. The big,

joyous laugh, the kind where she doubles over and slaps her leg, the one she did at a party and I instantly fell in love with her even though we'd never met.

I open the door, and she immediately composes herself. On her computer screen, I catch a brief glimpse of Bradley Hoof as I pass into the kitchen.

"My boyfriend is home," she says, and I can't place the tone. Is it a warning to her coworker to watch what he says? Is it to let him know why she is acting differently? Or is it disappointment? She hasn't even made eye contact with me yet.

I go into our bedroom, and I imagine what it would be like to take her hand and pull her out of her meeting and bring her here, to our bed and into our past, when we grappled and yanked and then held each other tightly.

My heart rate quickens, my fingertips quiver. I open the bottom drawer of my dresser and open an old condom box, where I stashed the ring I bought only a few weeks after we met. It's small but mighty. The lone diamond grabs at all the light in the room.

The meeting in the other room has ended. I hear my girlfriend moving around the apartment. Still clutching the ring in my hands, I kneel by the door and hold it out in front of me. My whole body shakes now. I look up expectantly, waiting for her to come in.

"I'm going out," she calls. "Will pick up food from my second-favorite restaurant."

Then the front door closes, and I remain there on one knee until gravity begins to crush me painfully into the floor.

#

When Bradley Hoof picks up my girlfriend outside our apartment, she climbs onto his back like a heroine in a romance novel. The wind, of course, perfectly tousles both of their hair.

We're going to eat at your second-favorite restaurant, Bradley

Hoof says. *You ready?*

I am naked and curled under a bench a few feet away. My girlfriend whispers and points at my disappointing penis, and then they both joyously laugh as they ride away.

I'm left to wonder how I ended up naked under a bench in this scenario. Still seems like it could happen though. Not too far out of the realm of possibility.

#

The next day, I'm outside the barn doors. It's time to defeat the myth. The ring is in my pocket, pressed against my leg. Like my girlfriend is right there with me. After I see Bradley Hoof, confirm his bipedal status, I will run home and propose. There will be much yanking and pulling in the bedroom. I will then continue my job search for real. It's a good plan that will begin the moment I press the bell.

So I press the bell.

Suddenly time stops. A bird hovers, frozen above me. A woman is half in and half out of a car across the street. The sound is sucked from the world. The only thing happening in the world is me, just me, waiting for the final Bradley Hoof to answer.

The intercom crackles to life. "Hello? Is someone there?"

"It's me. I'm here."

A pause.

"Yes, it's you," he says.

"I needed to meet you."

"I saw you too, outside the screen, during our meetings." More crackling from the intercom. "I wanted to ask your name. I thought about tracking you down, too."

The ring shifts in my pocket, and I no longer feel it pressing against my leg.

"Are you a centaur?" I ask.

"I will let you in," he says. "You will see."

The door begins to buzz loudly as if it has come to life. I

hesitate. If I go in, everything will change—I can feel it.

But if I go in, I'll finally know.

I'll finally know.

If I go in.

Tale #4: Silence

If a woman shows too often the Medusa's head, she must not be astonished if her lover is turned into stone.

— Henry Wadsworth Longfellow, "Table-Talk"

Irene and I had reached the point in our nascent relationship where we were pretty comfortable with each other, but we weren't sure if we could talk about constipation and back pimples and errant body hair yet. I had a key to her apartment, and she had a key to mine. Neither of us had used them.

Then her parents planned a visit.

"My mom will love you," Irene said, and she gave me that smile where she showed her entire top row of teeth with her eyes squeezed closed. I wanted to fold her up and tuck her into my chest forever.

It was Tuesday night, so we were at her apartment. I liked how her bed smelled like dryer sheets and her cat purred above our heads like a whirring fan blade. But we never had sex at her place because she was embarrassed her roommate would hear. I was convinced it was more embarrassing that her roommate thought we were abstinent in our early twenties, but that's why I lived alone. I didn't want to guess what a roommate was thinking.

"And what about your dad?" I said. I leaned back on her bed and felt truly comfortable. It was rare for me to feel so comfortable talking to someone. It's the main reason I wanted us to work out.

"He doesn't really talk," she said. "But I'll be able to tell if he likes you."

"Let's just say hypothetically that your dad doesn't like me?" I said.

"Then I guess we'd be through." She nudged me like it was a joke, but I knew she was serious. She always spoke about her dad in a hushed voice.

"Maybe I shouldn't meet him yet. It's too early, right? I haven't even told you about my time in prison and my intense addiction to online gambling. Oh, and the porn. So much porn."

Irene laughed and tucked her head between my shoulder and neck. "Very funny."

"You never know, it could be true," I said.

"If it is, you'll be sorry."

"Really?" I said. "Is that a sexy threat or a real threat?"

"It's real," she said with nary a glint in her eye.

I experienced a real sense of dread. Like knowing in advance a plane was going to crash and deciding to board anyway.

But then she smiled and everything was wonderful again.

"So it's official," I said, though I was officially terrified, "I'm meeting your parents. When is this fateful meeting happening?"

"Tomorrow," she said, her breath warm on my neck. "They arrive later in the afternoon. And they're crashing with me here for a week."

"Does that mean you won't be sleeping at my place tomorrow night?"

"Not a chance. My parents would freak out if they knew I did that."

"Want to have completely silent sex right now? And when I say silent, I mean your roommate will think I've gone home."

Irene laughed again. "Just this once."

#

I set an alarm so I could leave Irene's apartment early to give her time to prepare for her parents' arrival. And for her to erase all signs that I'd ever slept there at any point in the six months of our relationship.

As I dressed, I watched her pull a trash bag full of stuffed animals from her closet and then place each one delicately into position at the end of her bed. She brought out a board with inspirational quotes affixed with thumbtacks and propped it on her desk. Then she hung up a poster of a unicorn. It looked extremely out of place on her previously bare walls. The only decorating I'd ever seen Irene do was put a plant at the end of her desk that she didn't even notice had died until I'd pointed it out.

"What is all this?" I said.

"My dad's been buying me these since I was little. It's just for the week. I'll pretend like I keep them on display."

"Does he think you're fourteen years old?"

"Very funny."

"Is it, though?"

"Is it what?"

"Is it very funny?"

Irene lifted a pink sweater with a rhinestone unicorn on the front. "Well, maybe it's funny. But this sweater is hilarious."

"Oh wow," I said. "Have you ever worn that?"

She laughed. "I'm not going to answer."

"Probably better," I said.

"You just don't understand because you don't have a close relationship with your parents," she said.

That stung a little, even though I knew we were just bantering. I don't tell many people about how distant I feel from my family, and I didn't like her using it as ammunition.

"Is it actually close if you have to pretend to be someone you're not?" I said.

"I'm not pretending. I'd wear this sweater every day. I love this crazy thing. Maybe it's you I'm pretending for."

She smiled, and I smiled. Then she stopped smiling, and I stopped smiling.

Then I left.

#

While I waited for Irene's parents to descend on our lives, I decided to go to the movies. I hadn't gone out on my own in a few months, and as the lights dimmed in the theater, I thrilled at my aloneness. But within the first few minutes of the movie, I knew Irene would have hated it. She was pretty chill about most things, but she was snobby about movies. She would have said it was trite and garrulous, and I'd already forgotten what both of those words meant. I could feel her disappointment in my film choice as a weight next to me. As if she'd suddenly materialized in the darkened theater. I could feel her shoulder tightening in her seat.

I got up and moved to the row behind me, hoping to leave the specter of her behind, but Irene seemed intent on diminishing my enjoyment. So I laughed harder at the funny parts and cried louder at the sad parts and then staggered out of the theater two hours later, exhausted.

I bought a coffee and some kind of pastry with a dollop of lemon on top and consumed it so fast that my fingers tingled.

Then, whether I liked it or not, it was time to head back to Irene's.

Irene opened the door when I knocked, and I was surprised to see she wasn't in the unicorn sweater. She hugged me awkwardly around the neck like she was squeezing a tube of toothpaste. Then she tugged my upper arm, and I stumbled into the room with my head down as if I was introducing my burgeoning bald spot first.

Irene's mom grabbed my other arm, and suddenly I was supported by two generations of women who smiled the exact same way.

"What a treat!" Irene's mom exclaimed. "You didn't tell me he was so dashing!"

I am not dashing. Not even close.

"I dig him," Irene said and clutched my arm harder.

"Don't you just want to gobble him up!" Irene's mom said, continuing to blast out exclamation points like the T-shirt shooter at a baseball game.

"Luckily you won't have to do that. We have food on the way," Irene said. "I ordered from Dad's favorite restaurant."

"Of course you did, dear."

I finally got my balance as Irene guided me into her small front room. She had placed a sheet over her TV and stacks of books had magically appeared out of nowhere. I wondered what her roommate would think of all this.

"Nice to meet you," I said because I realized I hadn't said a word yet.

"This can't really be our first meeting!" Irene's mom said. "I feel like I already know you so well!"

"Mom, you're screaming again."

That's when I realized that Irene was embarrassed of her mom. Much as I'd always been embarrassed of my own mother. But Irene's mom, though rather blustery and maybe a touch disingenuous, seemed nice. Whereas my mom was a viper. You could tell she was mean the moment you met her, but you didn't know she'd drawn blood with her words until parts of you were strewn across the floor. I couldn't go anywhere with my mom without her getting into a verbal fight with someone. She felt that all strangers were placed in her path to ruin her day.

I also missed her quite a bit.

Irene's mom patted me on the arm. "I'm sure your friend can handle a robust voice." But she'd noticeably dropped her decibels.

"It's fine," I said. "I like the excitement. My life is generally very quiet. I need to get shaken up every once in a while."

Irene leaned toward me. "You don't have to try so hard. She likes you already."

"Okay," I said. But I didn't feel I'd been trying at all.

Irene left the room, and Irene's mom turned her gaze back to me. She suddenly seemed more intense. Aggressive, even. I felt under attack, and I had to look away from her.

"You ready for this?" she said.

"Not really," I said.

"Nobody is," Irene's mom said. "But you'll get through it. Maybe it will be like seeing the future."

A moment later, Irene pushed a wheelchair into the front room. And on that wheelchair sat the most amazing stone carving of a man I'd ever seen. Perfectly etched features with realistic shading and contouring. Delicate appendages that looked as if they could move on their own. The statue wore beige slacks and a pale blue silk shirt that was open at the collar, exposing a hint of excruciatingly carved chest. The stone eyes were full of intelligence and wit.

Irene looked at me. Her mom looked at me. The statue looked at me.

"Cool," I said because it was the only word that managed to assemble itself in the mushy recesses of my brain.

"What's cool?" Irene said.

I looked at Irene's mom expectantly looking at me. Then I looked at Irene expectantly looking at me. Then I looked at the cat licking its ass on the table. I had no idea what to say.

"That wheelchair seems like a lot of fun," I said.

"Seriously? I'm trying to introduce you to my dad."

"Oh yeah. That's cool too. Really cool. So *this* is your dad?" I could feel the front door calling from behind me, promising the sweetest of all escapes.

"The one and only," Irene's mom said.

I couldn't figure out if this was some kind of a joke or prank or somehow completely real. Based on the expression on Irene's face, I needed to choose soon.

"Nice to meet you," I said for the second time that day. But I said it really loud as if the sonic waves generated by my voice could penetrate the cold hard stone.

The statue's fixed expression looked pretty disappointed.

"He can hear you," Irene said. "Just fine."

"He just won't answer," Irene's mom said.

"Should I pretend he isn't a statue?" I said mostly to Irene's mom, but I was happy for an answer from anyone.

Irene shook her head. "Oh, so now you're the one pretending?"

"I didn't mean pretend," I said.

"Didn't you, though?"

And that's when the doorbell rang.

Irene turned to me. "That's the food. Would you mind grabbing it? Maybe you can pretend to be a fantastic tipper."

As she wheeled her dad over to the table, I opened the door to find a rather large man holding a greasy brown bag. To escape, I'd have to somehow get around him.

"Fifty bucks," he said.

That was my food budget for the week in one fell swoop. Plus, I had to be a fantastic tipper.

The man swiped my card, and I leaned closer to him and lowered my voice. "Say your girlfriend introduced you to her dad and he was made completely of stone. What would you do?"

"I don't have a girlfriend."

"Well, let's say anyone you have ever known in your life introduced you to their dad and he was made completely of stone."

"In this hypothetical situation, the person I know isn't made of stone?" the man said.

"No."

"I'd probably find out if it was contagious."

"Yes, good thinking," I said.

"Or if the person in your life, in your case, a girlfriend,

I guess . . ." He looked at me with a hint of distaste, as if it didn't seem possible I could have pulled that off. "You know," he started again. "If they somehow caused it."

#

When I returned clutching the greasy bag, Irene and her mom were sitting on either side of her dad at the small table. I stared at Irene's dad's face, looking for any sign that he was aware of his surroundings. If anything, he just seemed somehow more disappointed.

I decided in that moment that I would treat the statue like it had been created in honor of her father. That perhaps he'd died and this was the way the family had dealt with it. Then I could change Irene's mom's comments about him not answering as sad little jokes instead of the weird shit it seemed to be. I'd get through this, and then later I'd talk to Irene about grief and healthy ways to deal with the loss of a parent. Not that my mom and I had been successful when my dad died.

"Food's here," I said brightly.

Irene's cat suddenly appeared in the room and leapt onto Irene's dad's lap. It spun three times and then sat with a content sigh. Irene's cat had never once sat with me, and I had a working central nervous system and a heart that beat sixty-eight beats per minute and blood that traveled to all my extremities. Irene's dad was as supple as a granite countertop.

Then I faltered. Was it possible that somehow Irene's dad was actually in there?

"Dad loved this place last time he visited," Irene said and took the bag from me. It shook slightly in her grip, and I realized she was nervous. Which kind of irked me because I was the one thrown into this situation with literally no advance warning. How hard would it have been for Irene to say that her dad was made of stone before I met him?

Irene unwrapped a limp burger and placed it on a plate in

37

front of her dad. The cat looked interested for a second and then decided not to bother.

I watched her dad. I wondered what I would do if he suddenly started moving. If he picked up that shitty burger and started chewing it with gusto.

Irene handed a burger to her mom and then one to me. My stomach acids let me know they weren't prepared to accept any food by roiling in my abdomen.

"So last time you were here you ate all this burger?" I said, like a detective trying to catch a thief in a lie. "And your dad enjoyed it? And then said aloud to everyone that it was his favorite?"

Irene and her mom both had their burgers unwrapped, but no one was eating.

"Ask him yourself," Irene's mom said. "I can tell you this: It's not *my* favorite."

In this crazy dinner, it seemed Irene's mom was the most on my side. "What is your favorite place?" I said.

"I never bothered getting one because I knew we'd never eat there."

I tried to steer the conversation down another path. "How do you manage the sleeping arrangements here?" I asked. "Irene's room is so small."

"How do you know what Irene's bedroom looks like?" Irene's mom asked, her eyes suddenly blazing at me again. There was power in that gaze.

"Just a guess," I said, averting eye contact. "All the apartments around here have small bedrooms."

"Come on, Mom," Irene said. "Let it go."

"All I'm saying is that I didn't know this was an *intimate* friend," Irene's mom said.

"We're not intimate friends," Irene said. But she said it like she meant it. Like even though I knew mostly what she looked like naked—I had seen all her parts, just never all at the same time—we were still basically strangers.

"We're intimate-adjacent," I said. "I like your daughter a lot."

Irene's expression softened, like she remembered that she did actually like me and that, if I was given a chance, I might fight for our relationship. But I wondered if there was any way that Irene and I could survive the addition of our previous lives into our relationship. Was there any chance we were strong enough?

Irene's mom crossed her arms, and she suddenly looked taller. "*Intimate-adjacent* sounds like young person lingo for premarital sex!"

"Mom!" Irene yelled.

I looked to Irene's dad as if he might jump in to help, but as I already knew, he was still a fucking statue.

"Since this isn't going all that well for me," I said. "I'd like to say that the burgers look disgusting, and I'm not going to eat mine."

Irene and her mom froze, their battle forgotten. Then both of their heads pivoted toward me, identical expressions of shock on their faces. It went beyond being disappointed in what I'd said. They were disappointed in me as a person. They seemed to be saying that the only way I could live up to their expectations was if I were made of stone, too.

Then, with the most perfect timing, Irene's roommate Lianne arrived.

"I thought I smelled the best burger in town," Lianne said. She wore scrubs over hunched, exhausted shoulders.

Irene and her mom rebooted, wiping away the animosity and returning to their façade of normality.

"We got you one," Irene said and extracted another burger from the greasy bag.

"Thank you so much," Lianne said directly to Irene's dad. "I needed this."

"Rough day?" Irene asked.

"You have no idea. I'm off to bed now. Another double tomorrow."

"We'll keep it down," I said. "I know what a light sleeper you are."

"Yes, we've heard all about it," Irene's mom said, and it was a relief to have her gaze shifted away from me.

Lianne grimaced. "Please," she said. "You couldn't wake me if you tried."

I had reached the end of this journey. "Irene. I get it now. You're surrounding yourself with silence. Well, I'm not a stone person. I have opinions on stuff. If everything is going to stay intimate-adjacent with us, then maybe this isn't going to work out."

I looked at Irene's dad and maybe I was imagining it, but there was this hint of a smile on his stone lips. The cat kind of seemed like it was smiling too. I didn't look at Irene or her mom.

"I'll see myself out," I said.

#

I decided to watch the same movie I'd watched earlier. The specter of Irene never appeared in the theater, but it became apparent about ten minutes into the movie that it actually was pretty bad. Maybe even banal. Another word Irene liked to use to describe things. This time I wished we had seen it together. I craved her over-analyzation of films.

So I left.

As I emerged from a cloud of buttery tang in the lobby, I heard someone call my name. I turned to find a grown-up version of a girl who used to live next door to my family when I was a kid.

"I thought that was you," she said.

"Just slinking out of the movie theater," I said. "Didn't want anyone to know I'd gone alone."

"Guilty," she said. "I'm doing the same. No shame in my game."

"I guess I should embrace it too. Sorry if I offended you in any way."

"Not at all," she said. Then a smile took over her face to a degree that seemed like overkill, considering we hadn't been all that friendly back in the day. "How crazy that we ran into each other after all these years. How are you doing? How's your family?"

I thought suddenly of Irene's roommate and what a deep sleeper she apparently was. I wondered why Irene and I had to be so quiet. Not just during sex. But with everything.

"Do you want the truth?" I said.

The grown-up girl from my childhood balked, even going so far as to take two steps away from me, but I went on anyway.

"I'm not doing well at all. I just found out that my current relationship lacks intimacy. And her dad is an unnerving, judgmental statue who makes me feel as if I failed myself somewhere along the way and will never recover. And also, I haven't talked to my mom in years because of some stupid thing I'm holding on to and we may never speak again. Plus my dad is dead."

"I'm so sorry to hear that," the girl said, her face flickering through at least five emotional indicators.

"I'd be happy to hear about anything bothering you. I'll listen to it all. Tell me everything."

She walked away.

#

As I left the theater, I tried to remember exactly why I'd stopped talking to my mom. I still had the feeling of being angry. Of being slighted. The superior belief that my mom owed me an apology. But I couldn't remember how it started.

All that was left was the aftermath.

I was positive that given enough time, I wouldn't remember what had upset me so much earlier when I'd met Irene's parents. I would replace facts with a dull certainty that I'd been completely in the right. Maybe life was a series of aftermaths and by leaving the craters smoldering in my past, I was finding it difficult to move into the future.

Like maybe I needed to stop blaming my mom for everything. She was mean, but I could be petty. And I didn't need that pettiness right now with Irene and her family. If I wanted to cut through stone, I needed to sharpen my ability to adapt to a situation that made me feel I wasn't in control.

I thought of my empty apartment. A bed I never made. A refrigerator containing food that only I liked. Books that only I had read. Irene had called my apartment a shrine. She said everything seemed to be cemented in place, thus preserving it for future generations. She would tiptoe around the place, comically refusing to disturb anything. Calling herself an archaeologist when she'd excavate a television remote or a clean towel.

I didn't want to return home to that shrine to myself. I wanted to set things right. Who was I to judge Irene's relationship with her mom? Or her dad? Or the quality of his favorite burgers? Or the fact that her dad was a statue?

So, with the sun setting metaphorically behind me, I turned toward Irene's apartment.

#

It was night by the time I arrived at Irene's building. I looked up to the third floor but her bedroom window, which faced out to the street, was dark. I slipped into her building and made my way up the stairs.

The closer I got to her door, the slower I moved. I messed up most things. It stood to reason that I would mess up an apology.

But then I was there. The door impassive. Silence emanating from behind it. I took three big breaths, in through my nose and out through my mouth, and I raised my hand and knocked quietly.

I waited, my chest aching. A few moments passed. Maybe they hadn't heard me.

I looked to the side and found my hand still raised, my knuckles white. So I knocked louder this time.

Now I was anxious. No one moved inside the apartment. I knocked a few more times but it was pretty obvious they weren't there. They must have gone to Irene's favorite ice cream shop or that art gallery near her work. If I kept knocking, the only thing I'd accomplish would be to wake her roommate.

I leaned my forehead against the door, and that's when I heard it. A loud thump just on the other side. Like a body hitting the floor.

"Irene?" I said.

No answer.

That's when I remembered the key. The one I'd never used before. I had it tucked in the fold of my wallet. I extracted it, and before I had time to talk myself out of it, I slipped it into the lock.

For a moment, it didn't seem to work. The handle wouldn't turn. I thought how fitting it would be if I had the wrong key.

But then it notched into place, and I was in the dark apartment.

"Irene?"

I waited, breathing slowly, giving my eyes time to acclimate. Shadows began to turn into objects. The table. The stacks of books. The covered TV. Then a wheelchair on its side. A mass of darkness beside it.

Irene's dad was on the floor, still in a perfect sitting position, but on his side now. What had seemed like a powerful posture during dinner now looked like a child huddled in fear.

"You okay?" I said. In the deep shadows, I expected him to answer. I expected him to ask me for help.

Suddenly Irene's cat rubbed his side against my leg.

"Oh, hey, buddy," I said. "Did you somehow knock over that chair?"

He turned and rubbed his other side on me. I was shocked. He'd never shown any affection toward me. I almost started crying when I heard his purr rumbling in his chest.

Then he moved away from me and began rubbing against Irene's father. We were connected somehow now. I moved across the room to his huddled form. I didn't look at his face. I knew I'd see his embarrassment at his predicament. I wanted to spare him that.

Instead, I righted his wheelchair and squatted next to him. I slid both of my hands under his shoulders. He felt exactly how I thought he would, like a gigantic piece from my grandfather's chess set. He was heavy, but not quite as heavy as I expected, as if he'd been carved with stone organs as well. Like there were hollow spaces, too. I was able to get him back into his wheelchair, and then I sat across the table from him.

Irene's cat jumped into his lap again and got comfortable. Maybe he really had, somehow, knocked his chair over. Could I really believe that it wasn't some accident? That he had done it himself? That he was trying to escape, too?

"What happened to you?" I said to the statue of Irene's dad.

"He wasn't always like that," said a voice.

I nearly choked to death on my own shock.

"Lianne?"

"Sorry, didn't mean to startle you." She entered the room and sat at the table with us and began noisily eating a bowl of cereal. She looked over at Irene's dad. "He never talked much, but this is a whole other level."

"But what happened?"

She crunched loudly. "Relationships are rough, man. You have to figure out how much you're willing to change. How much you're willing to tolerate. Or will you be quiet forever?"

Irene's dad's expression had changed. Softened.

"Is that why you came back?" Lianne said. "Have you figured it out?"

"Figured out what?"

"You have to be able to say what's on your mind without looking away. You have to meet their gaze. It's like an opposite medusa?" Lianne took another bite of cereal and thought for a moment. "I don't know, maybe I'm just talking nonsense because I'm tired. But I've known Irene and her family a long time. We grew up together. I don't think she wants a relationship like her parents'. But you're going to have to speak up."

She let her spoon drop into her bowl and sighed. "I'm going back to bed."

I wasn't sure what to say. I wanted to thank her, even if I wasn't sure exactly what for. Not yet.

But I knew the thing I really wanted to ask would have to be left unsaid. I'd never know if she thought this statue was really Irene's dad.

"Are you really a sound sleeper?" I asked instead before she left the room.

"A train could drive through here and I'd sleep through it."

And then I was alone with Irene's dad again.

The silence was unbearable.

Part 2:
The Middle Reveals Problems

Tale #5: Where the Magic Is

"I've never really understood," the unicorn mused as the man picked himself up, "what you dream of doing with me, once you've caught me."

— Peter S. Beagle, *The Last Unicorn*

Maggie walked in with something wrapped in butcher's paper and placed it on the table with a flourish. "Unicorn," she said.

"Is that a new pet name for me?" I asked.

"It's what's for dinner."

Maggie and I had done plenty of kinky things over the years, almost always at her request, but we'd stayed away from eating rare, magical animals. Besides, I'd already warmed a slice of pizza in the microwave and had just sat down to eat. I'd even used a paper plate because I wasn't expecting her home so early. Maggie came down hard on creating unnecessary waste, but sometimes I wanted to throw something away and get on with my night.

"You think it's true what they say about eating unicorn?" she asked. "I don't know. I think I do, but maybe it's stupid." She lowered her eyes, embarrassed, as if we were just meeting for the first time. But then she couldn't help herself. "I'm sorry. Where did you get a paper plate?"

"I have a stash," I said. Which was true. I kept them in my sock drawer.

Her lips curved down to reveal the dimple at the top of her right cheek. No aphrodisiac or bedroom accouterments would ever turn me on more than that dimple. "So what do you think?" she asked.

"I think it would be easier to keep the paper plates in the kitchen."

"I'm talking about the unicorn."

I looked at the butcher's paper on the table between us, a purple stain spreading along the bottom. I'd seen parts of unicorn used before. After my parents divorced, my dad had begun mixing ground unicorn horn into his coffee to make him more virile. My mom had taken to wearing a lock of unicorn mane around her wrist to boost her confidence. When we were teenagers, my sister had even boiled a unicorn hoof and drunk the murky water to get some guy in her biology class to notice her. Everyone did those kinds of things at some point. But none of them were as macabre as this hunk of meat practically throbbing on the table. I wanted to scoop Maggie into my arms, like I would when we'd first started dating, like I could never be persuaded to let go, and tell her that we didn't need to eat unicorn meat to rekindle what we'd once had.

"How do you know it's actually unicorn?"

She rested her hands on the table. "How do we know that anything we buy is what it claims to be? That steak you like at the meat counter could be dog."

"If it is, it's good as hell."

Maggie plowed forward, anxious to get to the point. "I feel confident this is the real deal. The guy had horns for sale too. And hooves."

"That doesn't bother you?"

"As if it bothers you. I don't think you want it to be real."

"I'm sorry, Maggie. It just doesn't look very appetizing." Blood had seeped through the paper and was pooling on the table. A tendril of it was working its way toward my plate.

"It's not supposed to be appetizing."

"A rousing endorsement."

She suddenly looked sad, and I knew what she wanted me to say: That I was ready to eat unicorn meat with her. That I believed it would bind us together forever. What I wanted to say: That no one in a strong relationship bought unicorn meat. Her choice of dinner said more than the last six months of us drifting apart.

"Do the hair thing," I said instead.

"No."

"Come on."

She reached behind her and pulled her hair out of its ponytail. It fell onto her shoulders like the curtain at the end of a performance. She grinned at me with genuine affection, and my pulse quickened at the sight.

"You ready to go on this adventure with me?" she asked.

The blood had reached the paper plate where my pizza sat, shriveled and helpless. "That thing is really leaking," I said.

"It's not about eating the meat. It's about the blood. The blood is where the magic is. I got the bloodiest piece he had."

I'd never heard Maggie talk that way, and I wasn't sure if I liked it. There was something pleading in her tone and unashamedly vulnerable. She leaned toward the wall and dimmed the light.

"We don't even have to cook it," she said. "We can eat it raw. Right out of the paper." She fixed her gaze on me. "We need this."

Maggie was breathing heavily, her chest heaving, waiting for me to respond. Through the window behind her, I saw a faint white glow.

"What is that?" I asked.

She turned and saw it too. We moved to the window in unison and looked into our unkempt yard. Standing between the mailbox and the driveway was a unicorn. Its mane blew in a slight breeze, its horn glowing from where it protruded from its forehead. I'd never seen one in person before. It looked much more like a horse than I expected.

"I've heard of this happening," Maggie said, her voice hushed. She reached for my hand but settled for my sleeve. "It can smell the blood of its fallen comrade. It's mourning."

As we watched, another unicorn joined the first. Maggie squeezed my forearm with both hands. "They're beautiful."

Without even noticing their arrival, I suddenly saw six more dispersed around our yard. Under the basketball hoop I never used anymore. Next to Maggie's bird bath. Pacing in front of the garage. And they were all glaring through the window at us.

"I can't do this," I said.

She pulled me away from the window. "Yes, you can."

By now, the blood had completely saturated the paper plate, and its edges drooped to the table. A faint glow came from inside the butcher paper, pulsing slightly, as if it were breathing too. Maggie reached over and began unwrapping it.

If I ate a piece of this unicorn with her, I'd be sending a message. And I wasn't sure what I wanted. Maggie was wonderful, but I wasn't sure she was my kind of wonderful anymore. I liked pizza. I liked paper plates.

"What about the unicorns outside?" I asked.

"Forget about them." She'd finished unwrapping the meat, and the glow filled the kitchen.

Glass shattered behind us. It sounded exactly like a horn striking a window.

"We have to hurry," Maggie said. "Before they take it from us."

The sound of more breaking glass came from the back of the house. Hooves on the tile in the bathroom. A whinny from our bedroom. We were surrounded.

"This doesn't seem right," I said.

"The dangerous things are the only things worth doing."

She put her fingers into the meat and pulled off a bloody piece. I could feel the unicorns watching me now, but I didn't want to turn around.

I wanted to live in that moment forever. Waiting for the feel of a horn through my shoulder blade. Maggie reaching out to me, blood dripping on the table. Our pulses pounding in unison. I felt more alive than I had in months.

Which is how mistakes are made.

Tale #6: Therapy

At supper that evening the usual conversation occurred about the unearthly sounds, but as not one of them could offer an explanation they concluded it was too deep a matter for them to talk about [. . .].

— Walter Hubbell,
The Great Amherst Mystery: A True Narrative of the Supernatural

Laura had been saying I had a bad attitude since our journey of reconciliation began over a year ago. But I couldn't see how staying the night in a haunted house was going to fix anything.

"When Dale and Rose stayed there," Laura said, "blood dripped from the walls and spiders crawled over the floors and the two of them huddled together the whole night. When the sun came up, their relationship was stronger than it had ever been."

We were on our backs on the bed, our shoulders almost touching. I couldn't tell if this was turning into another earnest late-night discussion or a fight.

"What do you think of that?" she asked.

"Are you hoping that happens when we stay there?" I asked. "Because that sounds awful."

"Which part?" she said, as if she were about to catch me

in a trap.

"The blood, Laura. The blood sounds like the worst part."

I turned to look at her and was reminded again of how beautiful she was in profile. The nose she detested, with its little ridge in the middle, made me want to work things out with her more than any session with our therapist ever could.

The thing was, we'd started this journey of reconciliation together, but I had no idea what we were trying to reconcile. All we knew for certain was that our relationship had previously meant something to us, and maybe it could mean something again in the future. But currently, we were both in unspoken agreement that it was a bit of a dud. I'm the one who called it our "journey of reconciliation" as a joke, but the name had stuck. Even the therapist called it that now. I hated when a joke was taken away from me and turned serious.

The role-playing was the worst. I would become Laura and she would become me while the therapist tapped her pen across her notebook. Laura did this impression of me where she stooped her shoulders and mumbled her words.

"You aren't listening," she'd say as me. "You don't get where I'm coming from."

And maybe I did say that a lot. It's not like either of them seemed anxious to know where I was coming from. My perspective didn't seem to matter at all.

The therapist would then wave in my direction, and I'd straighten my back and say as Laura, "You never take out the trash before it overflows onto the kitchen floor, and you never put the toilet seat down, and you eat the ice cream directly out of the container instead of getting a bowl."

Laura would shake her head vigorously, as if I was the most disappointing thing in her life, and then she and the therapist would share a "moment" where she'd telepathically say, *Can you believe what I'm dealing with here?* and the therapist would telepathically say back to her, *Get out while you can.*

I'm not stupid. I know it's not about the nagging. If everything was great with Laura, like it had been at the beginning of our marriage, then my tolerance level would be much higher, and I probably wouldn't do all those things on purpose.

The point was that at one time Laura didn't care about those things. And now she did. A lot. Like she was mimicking some lady she followed on Instagram or she was reading some shitty blog. Also she was addicted to therapy and the mumbo jumbo that came along with it. She apparently even had a love language, and she wanted to know what mine was. That shit mystified me because a few years ago, if we'd heard someone talking about their love language, we would have made fun of them. The hardest part about everything was that I was told I had a bad attitude, by Laura and the therapist, because I wasn't accepting Laura's changes. But it seemed perfectly okay that nobody accepted that I wanted to stay the exact same.

Now Laura wanted to try this horror therapy.

"How do we know spending the night with a poltergeist is safe?" I asked.

"Putting your heart out there is never safe," she said.

Anything I said in response would make me sound like an asshole, so I said, "Let's do it."

The next morning, as we crunched cereal at the table, Laura smiled, and it made me feel giddy. I hadn't seen that smile in months.

"I didn't think you'd agree to it," she said.

"I'm committed," I said. I reached across the table and brushed my fingers along hers, but she pulled away.

"We should pack for tonight."

I nodded. "Any tips? Should I bring extra underwear?"

She stared at me.

"In case I shit my pants, right?"

"This isn't a joke," she said.

"I know that. Yeah. I joke when I'm scared."

"Just go pack."

#

1321 South Cramden Street was a regular house in a regular neighborhood with neighbors a little too close on either side and a perfectly cut yard. The housing development was only five years old, which seemed way too young to have a poltergeist. How angry could a ghost be if he'd lived somewhere with central air and skylights?

After all her big talk, Laura was near-shaking nervous. She sat in the passenger seat of our station wagon and stared at the unassuming one-story house.

"Does it give off a vibe or anything to you?" she asked.

I wasn't sure what answer she was looking for. "Not yet."

"Okay then," she said and opened the car door. I grabbed our bags from the back seat and followed her up the sidewalk to the front door.

"Are we supposed to knock?" I asked.

Laura's dark brown eyes opened wide. "I have no idea."

I shrugged and knocked loudly on the heavy oak door. The sound echoed into the house, but nothing stirred.

"How about this?" I said. "If it's unlocked, we stay. If it's locked, we get the hell out of here and go get some ice cream."

"Deal," she said. It felt nice to agree on something.

I turned the handle, and the door swung open to reveal a charming house. Wood floors. Big windows that let in tons of light. A fireplace and an open kitchen. Everything Laura had wanted in our dream home, back when we had dreams. If only we were here house hunting and not trying to scare our relationship back to life.

Laura walked in as if we were about to put in a bid. All her previous fear was gone.

"Can you imagine?" she said.

"Yes," I said. But I bet we were thinking of different things. I was imagining chasing her through the house naked and making out in every single room.

I shuffled into the house behind her and was surprised by the thick coating of dust on the floor. Supposedly, hundreds of couples had come here hoping to save their relationships, but I didn't see a single footstep or a fingerprint smudge near any of the light switches. As if no one had been here in years.

"I thought you said this house was booked solid every day. That we were lucky this spot happened to open."

"We were," Laura said sharply.

I dropped our bags on the floor and walked past her, dust billowing behind me. "Where are we supposed to sleep? Or sit down? There's no furniture."

Laura rubbed her temple in the way I always loved, like she was stimulating her brain to work harder on a problem. "We'll improvise," she said, which I knew was a dig at me because that's what I always said. She was getting too good at the role-playing stuff.

"You're telling me Dale and Rose slept on the floor?" I said. "Dale won't even ride in the back seat of a car."

Laura moved toward the kitchen like she already owned the place. "Maybe they were too terrified to notice there was no furniture."

I scanned the eggshell white walls and the wood baseboards. There was no sign that these walls ever had blood on them. There wasn't even a single spider web. It was starting to feel like we'd been duped. I knew exactly what was going to happen. We were going to stay up all night in an empty house and talk about our relationship.

"Well, I'm going to the bathroom before this poltergeist gets started," I said and left Laura in the kitchen opening and closing the mahogany cabinets. I walked down the hall and dust continued to explode around me. The first door I opened had a small toilet and a sink inside. I went in, shut the door, and paused to take a deep breath.

What I wanted to say but had been too scared through the entire year of therapy, was that I didn't have a problem with the fact that Laura wanted to change or grow or whatever. I was totally fine with it. The problem was that I wasn't one hundred percent on board with the new, improved Laura. This new, enlightened Laura who was bothered by everything I did. By everything I said. Who no longer laughed at my jokes. Who gave the impression that she'd moved past me and that I would never catch up.

After I finished pissing, I let the lid slam loudly so Laura could hear it in the other room. I stared at myself in the mirror as I washed my hands. I looked determined, which was good. I looked like someone prepared to see this journey all the way to the end. Which I think Laura deserved. But I did have to admit that she was right; I no longer looked like the guy she'd fallen in love with. She'd said that during our last session, and I'd stared at her even though she was unable to meet my eyes, and I realized she still looked exactly like the girl I had fallen in love with.

I splashed some water on my face and wondered what was going through her mind out there in the kitchen. Did she really think this house could fix anything?

Something moved in the corner behind me. Just a shimmer, but enough to give my heart a jolt. I leaned toward the mirror and watched a shadow peel away from the wall like a Band-Aid.

"I'm the poltergeist," a crinkly voice said.

"I can't believe you're actually real," I said.

The poltergeist sounded wounded. "You don't believe in poltergeists?"

"I do. It was just you I doubted," I said.

"Because this was Laura's idea, right?"

"You got me there," I said, and I felt pretty shitty about it.

The shadow leaned a little closer, and I tightened my shoulders.

"You need to stop always expecting failure," he said.

"I hear you," I said, but he was making me full-on uncomfortable now. "Are you only in the mirror?"

"Oh, right. Spoiler alert. If you turn around, there will be nothing behind you."

I finished washing my hands, but there was no towel.

"Fresh out of towels, buddy. Use your jeans," the poltergeist said.

"Laura hates when I do that."

"It'll be fine," he whispered and reached toward me. I felt a cold breeze on my neck, and it finally struck me that I should be terrified.

"Are things about to get scary?" I said.

The poltergeist laughed. "What do you think?"

"I think this is going to be too much for Laura. Maybe we could ease into the terror? Let her warm up to it a bit."

"Who's in charge around here?" the poltergeist bellowed.

I closed my eyes and gritted my teeth, ready for the walls to start bleeding. I waited. I listened. Nothing.

Then I heard stifled laughter, as if the poltergeist was clamping his hand over his mouth. "You should see your face," he said.

I slowly opened my eyes, and it was true: my reflection in the mirror looked ridiculous. Like the picture taken at the top of a roller coaster. Just a few weeks ago, Laura had told the therapist that she was still upset that we hadn't bought the picture of us at the top of Zoom Mountain when we went to an amusement park not long after we were married. I don't even remember the "picture incident," as Laura called it, but apparently, I'd said it was a waste of money.

"We looked so young, so pure," Laura had said. "Scared to death of the upcoming drop. It perfectly encapsulated our relationship. I wanted that picture so much, and he didn't understand what it meant to me. That was where it started."

"I think you're putting a little too much emphasis on this picture," I'd said in my defense. "It probably cost like thirty bucks. And we were probably screaming."

But right now, I'd do anything to get that photo for her. I suddenly felt the sadness she must have felt. We both knew that not only did that photo no longer exist, but neither did that moment.

The poltergeist cleared his throat. "Whoa, lost you there," he said. "You know, it's considered rude to space out when a poltergeist is attempting to terrify you."

"Oh, God. I'm so sorry," I said. I started to turn from the mirror.

"Ah ah ah. You can only see me in the mirror, remember?"

So I was forced to continue staring at myself and the dark shadow of the poltergeist hovering behind me like a cloud of bad ideas.

"This is how things are going to work. I'm going to start by asking each of you what would scare the other the most."

I couldn't help it. I groaned.

"What now?"

"It's more role-playing."

The poltergeist growled. Every single hair on my body stood up.

"I'm sorry. I know you're doing your best here." Then it hit me. "Wait a minute. Did you already ask Laura? Did she say I'd be scared of more role-playing?"

The poltergeist snickered. "I don't know, did I?"

Now I was angry again. "So you can literally do anything?"

"Anything."

I thought about this, watching the shadow stretch like a rubber band. I really wanted to come up with an idea that would scare Laura the most.

"I got it," I said. "You should tell her she has to accept me as is. That would scare the shit out of her."

The poltergeist made a loud yawning sound. "Could you be more boring?" Then he laughed and disappeared.

I spun from the mirror, but there was no sign that he'd ever been there. I couldn't help feeling like I'd failed the first test. I wiped my hands on my jeans and opened the door.

Laura was standing on the other side. "Anything?" she asked.

"You didn't hear all that?"

"All what?"

"I just talked to the poltergeist."

Laura narrowed her eyes, but she craned a little to the left so she could see into the empty bathroom. "I wish you'd take this seriously. I had high hopes going into this."

"I really did talk to him," I said. "He wasn't that bad, to be perfectly honest. Actually seemed kind of open-minded."

"You're a dick." She pushed past me into the bathroom. "And would it have killed you to put the toilet seat down?"

I looked past her and sure enough, that crazy poltergeist had put the toilet seat up. "The haunting has begun," I said.

She shut the bathroom door.

It wasn't until I returned to the front room that I noticed something strange. Laura had left no footprints in the dust while I could see every step I'd taken since walking in. It was like I had come here alone.

While I waited for Laura, I wandered from room to room. When I entered the master bedroom, which was pretty stellar with a skylight and two walk-in closets, it occurred to me that the poltergeist was probably talking to Laura.

I went back to the bathroom and put my ear against the door. I didn't hear anything.

"Laura."

Nothing.

I knocked.

Still nothing.

I opened the door onto an empty bathroom.

"Laura?" I backed into the front room. With her suddenly gone, I could feel the emptiness of the house. The unmoving air. The missing weight of Laura's hopes and disappointments that had become part of my fabric.

This felt like she was gone forever.

A face appeared in the dust on the floor like a child had drawn it with his finger. "You okay?" the poltergeist asked, the dust mouth moving as best as it could to form words.

I squeezed my eyes closed. "Is Laura dead? Did you kill her?"

The poltergeist laughed. I was sick of all his laughing.

"She's not dead," he said. "She's over there by the window."

I turned and found no sign of her.

The poltergeist chuckled. "I split reality in half. You're both here, but neither of you can see each other. Pretty cool, right?"

"That's why I can only see my footprints."

"Yeah. It's like that biblical allegory. But I'm not planning to carry you at any point, so don't get your hopes up."

I glanced around the empty room. "Now what?"

"You wait," he said, and then the face blew away in a small breeze, as if someone had left the door open.

I moved to the window, hoping to feel some sign of Laura. Maybe if we were standing in the exact same spot, we would suddenly be in sync again. I tried to look where I thought she'd be looking. I watched a young boy ride his bike up and down the street, unsteady, as if he'd only recently taken off his training wheels. It's interesting how many crutches we are given as we go through life, all to keep us upright and moving forward.

My crutch was sarcasm, of course. And I was ready to fully admit that I hadn't been serious about this journey of reconciliation. But I could change that. Maybe we were going to make it. Maybe we weren't. It was entirely possible that we just didn't like each other anymore. It was a scary thought that I'm sure was brought on by proximity to a poltergeist, but definitely possible. Maybe it didn't matter what we did. Because I owed Laura a real attempt. That much I could give her.

"Hey, poltergeist," I said.

"Whattup?"

I couldn't tell where his voice was coming from. "Can you send a message to Laura for me?"

"No can do."

It had gotten dark now, and the house seemed a bit more menacing. Any one of the gathering shadows could peel away from the wall at any time.

"I know you have a plan and all. But just tell her, from me, that I might not be able to change in the way she wants me to, but that I'm ready to truly begin the journey. Tell her I don't need to role-play anymore. I think she'll know what I mean."

"I can't do it, man."

"I won't try to change any of your other plans tonight," I said. "Just do this one thing for me."

"She left," the poltergeist said with a loud exhale of breath. "I've been trying to figure out how to tell you for the last hour or so."

"I don't believe you."

"Trust me, I was as surprised as you. She even thanked me for showing her a reality without you in it."

I didn't want to believe him, but I did. I couldn't feel her anywhere in the house. I truly was alone. I lay back on the hardwood floor and closed my eyes.

"What are you doing?"

"Sleeping," I said.

"Oh. I figured you'd be heading out now. I was hoping for an early night."

"Nope," I said. I wanted to understand the emptiness before I left. I wondered if Laura and I would forever be in different realities even outside this house, never to cross paths again. Because maybe, if I really stopped to think about it, we were always on different paths. Maybe the roller coaster was never a good analogy for our relationship precisely because we were sitting next to each other and going down the same track.

The poltergeist was right next to me now, breathing loudly, but I'm not sure how I knew that because I still couldn't see him.

"What would I have to do to get you out of here?" he asked.

I thought about how the poltergeist had already accomplished what I'd imagined would scare me most, and yet I was still here. "You could make the walls bleed," I said.

"Done."

Tale #7: Remnants

Bigfoot was interviewed on *The Patty Winters Show* this morning and to my shock I found him surprisingly articulate and charming.

— Bret Easton Ellis, *American Psycho*

"There it is again," Ginny said, her head lifted slightly off her pillow, as if the sound of our garbage cans clattering onto the driveway needed to enter both of her ears at the same time.

"I think we should throw away more stuff so they're heavier," I said. This was the third week in a row that our cans had been knocked over in the night.

"Or you could go out there and see what's causing it."

"I just got in bed," I said. Ginny's lawyer TV show had ended before I was done updating my resumé, so she'd gone to bed without me. After she'd left, I stayed up watching risqué late-night programming, hoping that someone would get naked. Nobody did.

"I'll go out and see what it is," Ginny said. But she made no move to get up because she knew exactly what I was going to say.

"Please, stay in bed," I said in my worst Shakespearean actor impression as I got to my feet. "I'll go. But don't move until I return, because the moonlight is perfectly illuminating your beautiful face."

She threw a pillow at me. "You sound like a romance novel."

I shrugged my shoulders. "Job hunt is a bust. I should write romance novels instead. Okay, while I'm out there, start brainstorming all the clever names I could give to people's bits and pieces."

"Lady parts have the best names. Good luck trying to find something non-aggressive to call boy junk. Everything sounds like something a Roman gladiator would yell before killing a tiger."

"I'm going outside now."

"Good," she said. I leaned over the bed to kiss her, but she rolled away and pulled the covers over her head with a laughing snort.

The thing is this: Everything in our relationship felt great. She was truly my best friend. I could even fart around her. And not just the covert ones. But at some point a few months ago, I began to notice her avoiding physical contact. She'd make a joke about pushing me away or covering her head or ducking past me while I was left puckering my lips like someone calling for their dog in the park behind our house. I just wanted her to squeeze my arm or give me a kiss on her way out of the room. I wanted it to feel like she was always checking to make sure I was still there. Because that's how I felt about her.

"Will you wait up for me?" I said.

"If you're lucky."

And there it was. Another joke.

#

The night was cool. Our driveway was perfectly parallel with the driveways of the four connected townhomes on either side. Everyone's cans were out on the curb. Ours were the only ones knocked over.

It was completely quiet.

I looked down the street one way and then the next. I looked up into the sky. I looked once more at the cans in the other driveways. Investigation complete. I wasn't some kind of garbage night Sherlock Holmes.

I'd left our bedroom light on upstairs in the hopes that Ginny would stay awake, but when I turned to walk back inside, I saw that our window was dark. I wondered what I'd done wrong. It could have been the lack of job. But I was trying incredibly hard. Writing people that I hadn't spoken to in over a decade. Constantly updating my online profiles with fancy new lingo I learned from looking at other people's profiles. And so many applications. Hundreds of them. Ginny seemed so supportive, but maybe it was a turn-off? It's not like they produced calendars featuring hot, unemployed guys for all the single ladies out there. The word "unemployed" never landed gracefully.

I had just decided I'd give the late-night program another chance before returning to bed when one of the garbage cans rattled on the pavement behind me. I spun around, but nothing was there. A chill passed through me. Something was watching me. Waiting. We didn't have bears or wolves or anything like that, but my mind began to frantically serve up options in which I was brutally torn apart by multiple wild animals, including some truly exotic ones from across oceans.

Then, as I watched in absolute horror, the shadow of one of the toppled cans stretched like taffy, pulling away from the can and hovering above it. The shadow had a head and broad shoulders. And it was breathing.

"Hello?" I said, because there wasn't a single brave word in my head.

A loud huff.

The shadow moved away from the cans, long, loping arms appearing. As it approached the streetlight, I saw its body was covered in matted red fur.

Bigfoot had knocked over our cans.

He moved slowly as if expecting me to run in fear. He clutched something dark and lumpy under his armpit. For some reason, he didn't seem threatening at all. He looked sad.

My curiosity about Bigfoot's intent was too much to bear. "What do you have there?" I said.

Bigfoot stopped in the middle of the street and stared at me. His low forehead made it impossible to tell if he was angry or not. He held the little bundle out in front of him. It had a slightly human shape, but no structure holding it together. He took a few steps closer.

The light caught it, and I saw it was made from clumps of Ginny's hair and her make-up remover pads and the other stuff she sloughed off over the course of a week. Bigfoot had made a person-shaped thing from it all. A Ginny-shaped thing.

He pointed up to our window. "Jee-knee," he grunted. He hugged the hair creature and it broke apart, bits of hair falling to the street. Suddenly he was on his knees, crying. He clawed at the asphalt until the wreckage was heaped in a ball.

Even though he was clearly hung up on my girlfriend, I couldn't muster any anger or jealousy or any of the emotions I was meant to feel. What I saw was a creature not unlike me. Craving a bit of intimacy. From Jee-knee.

"I'll help you," I said and approached Bigfoot with my hands out, palms facing him. The universal sign that I've never started, or won, a fight in my entire life.

Bigfoot grunted and hunched his body over the pile of hair, protecting it as his tears fell in enormous splashes. I moved next to him and placed my hand on his back. He was warm and solid. He was vibrating with sobs.

"This isn't that bad," I said. "We can fix this." He looked up at me, and it was a bit of a shock. His face was double the size of mine.

"Bring it over here." I mimed picking up the hair pile in my arms, and he got the idea. We moved together toward the upended trash cans.

I pointed to the ground, and Bigfoot lay the pile gently on the driveway. As he was reshaping it, I began digging through our trash. I found the remains of our takeout Chinese food and soggy coffee filters. I thought about Ginny's and my life together and how I could see it all laid out here on the ground. It felt intimate, all our detritus entwined like that.

"You need more hair," I said. "And something to keep it all together."

Then he held up a pregnancy test. I could see in the dim light that it was negative, which was a relief. But the problem was that Ginny and I hadn't had sex in almost three months.

"You stay here," I said to Bigfoot and he snorted at me again. "I'll be right back."

#

I read somewhere once that cockroaches liked to be touched. I can't remember anything else in the article. The idea that a cockroach had desires, and one of those desires was to be caressed, had punched a little hole in my heart that was still there now. Unable to be filled. And now, as I moved into our home and up the stairs, I felt the same bond with a creature who, until about fifteen minutes ago, I hadn't thought existed.

When I returned to our room, I was surprised to find Ginny facing the door with her eyes open. The light from the hallway illuminated the lower half of her body, which was covered by our quilt. I could picture her elbows tucked into her sides, her knees drawn up above her waist. A perfect circle.

"What was it?" she said.

"Bigfoot," I said.

"Not again," she said and sat up abruptly. Her long black hair fell onto her shoulders like waves crashing on the shore.

"What do you mean, not again?"

"This is the second time he's tracked me down." She gritted her teeth as if it hurt to form the next words. "I was just nervous, okay. It was right before you and I moved in together. I had a small freak-out. I was scared. Of the commitment. I saw him a few times. It didn't mean anything to me. He tracked me down just before I moved out of my apartment, and I thought once I was gone, once I'd moved in with you, that would be the end of it."

Here she was confessing her infidelity, very casually, with no sense of culpability. And it was obvious she didn't feel bad about what she'd done or think that it was something I should feel bad about either. For her, the problem was that the guy, or, in this case, Bigfoot, had returned. I was surprised to discover that the anger pulsing through me was on behalf of Bigfoot. Because of course his time with Ginny had meant something to him. She was amazing.

"I don't know how he found me again," she said.

"He probably has a great sense of smell," I said dumbly.

"I'm sure he does." She sighed. "Are you mad?"

"I will be," I said. "When it settles in. Why Bigfoot?"

"Because he was different from every other person in the world."

Ginny and I had moved in together over a year ago. If she hadn't seen Bigfoot since then, I couldn't figure out the math on why there was a pregnancy test in our garbage can now.

"Would you do me a favor?" she said.

Of course I would do her a favor. She knew that there was no end to the favors I would do for her.

She took a deep breath and looked me directly in the eyes. "Would you tell him to leave? Tell him to never come back. Tell him we're happy. Tell him to forget about me."

Was this the way she would break up with me one day? Would I find out she was *happy* with someone else?

"No problem," I said. "I'll take care of it."

#

I returned to the front door and watched Bigfoot moving deftly in the darkness. Tenderly selecting pieces of Ginny and adding to his pile.

When he looked up and saw me watching, he waved me over to join him.

I opened the door, not sure what to say to him. "Hey, man."

Bigfoot grunted and patted the sides of his head like he was styling an imaginary head of hair. All the while staring at me. His face wrinkled and serious. It was hard to imagine him with Ginny. But unfortunately, it was hard to imagine me with her too. Soon it would be me out here with the trash cans.

Bigfoot grunted louder now, his hand gestures becoming more exaggerated.

"I'll see what I can fish out of the shower," I said.

I walked slowly back to the room and heard Ginny's level breathing. It was hard to believe she'd fallen asleep so quickly, especially without knowing the outcome of the Bigfoot situation.

"Ginny," I said.

She didn't move. Her breathing never faltered.

I stomped loudly into the bathroom and began knocking over her bottles of lotions and creams and deodorants. They clattered into the sink. Then I swung open the shower curtain. It reverberated on the shower rod like an impending storm. I knelt and pulled a small tuft of her hair from the drain.

Not nearly enough.

That's when I spotted the pair of pink-handled scissors on the back of the toilet. I snatched them up with no immediate thought as to what they might accomplish. They just felt good in my hand. They felt like an answer.

I moved back into the room. "Ginny," I said.

A long inhale.

I leaned onto the bed, the mattress squeaking gently. "I found the pregnancy test."

A long exhale.

Her hair was splayed on the pillow behind her. I ran my fingers through it, smoothing it into an upside-down question mark.

Then I tucked her hair between the blades of the scissors.

"You can do this," she said without moving. "But only once. Then we're even."

But I didn't want to get even. I wanted us to *be* even. I wanted her to talk to me. I could forget about Bigfoot and the pregnancy test and the weeks of her pushing me away if only we could agree to move forward again together.

I pulled the scissors away from her hair and placed them on the nightstand. "Bigfoot's gone," I said. "He's never coming back. When he saw how happy I was, he understood. He's a reasonable fellow. I mean, he looked happy for me to be so happy. We were just so happy out there. Just two happy guys feeling happy for each other." I paused after this rudimentary soliloquy. "And now he's gone. And it's just us, Ginny. It's just us."

Her eyes remained closed.

Tale #8: Waves

I have heard the mermaids singing, each to each.
I do not think that they will sing to me.

       — T. S. Eliot, "The Love Song of J. Alfred Prufrock"

It's true. I bought a ring. And it was exactly to Sharon's specifications.

A few hours before our dinner reservation, where I was going to proffer the ring and Sharon was going to pretend she had never seen it before in front of a room full of strangers, I drove south until the highway was only a few hundred feet from the ocean. We'd gotten so caught up in planning this dinner, including prewriting the captions for our inevitable Instagram posts and practicing the pause after I'd gotten on one knee, so that people at the other tables might think Sharon was going to say no, that we never talked about anything important. Like for starters: What was going to happen next?

I parked on the shoulder of the highway and picked my way over rocks until the roar of the ocean drowned out any idea of my own significance. I got as close as I could to the violence of the water and stared into the void, clutching the ring in my right hand. Then, and only then, did I scream into the waves as if my shredded vocal cords could stop the future.

When I was done, I sat on a rock and thought about what I'd order for dinner.

That's when I heard a woman's voice buried in the silence between waves. "Screaming Guy! Are you still over there?"

"Yeah," I said, not necessarily pleased with my new moniker. In life, away from this rocky beach, I was praised for my level-headedness. My ability to stay calm in any situation. Sharon knew she could count on me to facilitate any task she set forth. Always to her exact specifications. Like with the engagement ring. And this dinner tonight.

"I'm flipping stuck," the woman said with some chagrin.

"What do you mean stuck?" I said.

A wave crashed and we both waited.

"It's all your fault," she called. A large rock formation was turbulently piled between us, as if flung there by the son of a sea god with too much time on his hands. There was no way to go around it without splashing into the ocean or climbing back up to the highway and then working my way down the other side. This woman was stuck and needed my help, of course, but it was difficult not to decry my rotten luck. I came to this desolate strip to be alone, and it was bordering on assault to discover another person here.

"My fault?" I said.

"I heard you screaming and thought you needed help. Now I'm stuck trying to reach you. Ironic, right?"

"I don't know about ironic," I said.

"What?"

"I said it's not that ironic."

"Just climb over here and help me, Screaming Guy."

I got to my feet as another wave detonated on the shore and stepped toward the pile of rocks. If Sharon were here, she'd have a plan for this. She'd have very strong opinions on where I would start my climb and which rocks to use for support. There were many times when having someone else do the steering for me suited me just fine. But there were a few things, especially lately, where I'd been scared to assert my influence. As if by agreeing to be steered, I'd also agreed to be silent.

"Are you still there?"

"I'm still here." After trying a few options, I discovered a good foothold and pulled myself along a crevasse that I'm sure Sharon would have thought too dangerous. And then I was at the top, looking down on a shallow pool. This side of the formation had a nice, gentle slope, and I carefully picked my way down without thinking too much about the best places to step.

The woman's golden hair came into view first. Then her bare shoulders. She twisted to face me, and I was unnerved by how much she resembled my girlfriend before Sharon. The one who still had my dog and, if I was honest, a starring role in some of my fantasies. She sat in the middle of the shallow pool and was busy tugging on a rock in a vain attempt to lift herself out.

"There you are," she said, a little breathless.

"Here I am," I said.

"I thought you'd look different," she said.

"How so?"

"I don't know. More screamy or something."

I wasn't sure how to respond to that.

"Well, are you going to help me?"

I splashed into the pool and hooked my arms around her waist. She leaned her head onto my shoulder and looked directly into my eyes. It was uncanny how I felt I knew this woman. Like she'd been part of my life at some point.

"Are you planning to lift me out or are we posing for our prom photo?"

I lifted her from the pool, and that's when I noticed her breasts were exposed. I almost dropped her.

"Pardon me," I said and quickly averted my eyes.

"Grow up. They're just boobs."

"I know what they are," I said. But now I was more focused

on the fact that she was definitely stuck. Something was holding her in the water. I gave her a good yank, and she yelped in pain.

"Be careful."

"I can't see what's going on under the water. What are you stuck on?" My back ached under the strain of holding her.

"If I knew, I'd do something about it."

"Wrap your arms around my neck," I said. "Then I'll count to three."

She spun as best as she could in my arms, and I suddenly found my nose buried in her hair. She smelled like salt and something citrus. Actually, she smelled exactly like the drink I got at the Applebee's bar whenever I told Sharon I was working late.

I pulled as hard as I could, and there was a horrific ripping sound. The woman let go of my neck and landed with a thud on the sand outside the shallow pool. After another wave crashed, I realized she was screaming now.

"I thought you were going to count to three!"

"I'm so sorry. I forgot."

"I'm bleeding," she said. "A lot."

I looked down and discovered she had a tail. I was so shocked that my fingers went numb. The tail shimmered an iridescent green in the mist. A deep gash sliced through the scales on the left side, from which quite a lot of blood poured. I'm not sure which discovery made me weaker, but I fell to the ground next to her. Waves crashed on the shore and sprayed across the rocks.

"Now what?" she said, sprawled and gasping on the sand. Then she passed out.

I half-carried and half-dragged her along the slippery rocks, her body completely limp the entire way. I tried my best to ignore the tail. And the blood.

She was a mermaid, of course. Which, fifteen minutes ago, was the strangest thing I'd ever encountered in my life. But now I was lugging a mermaid to my car, sweating and aching as the sun reappeared from behind the clouds to watch the spectacle and the waves continued to guffaw. If Sharon were here, she'd have no doubt that my gym membership had gone unused for months. I was panting hoarsely and had to stop every few feet to rest. Sometimes the mermaid's head slumped forward and sometimes it lolled back, her face still giving me that sense of déjà vu.

She was real. That was certain. But there was no more magic. She was just a heavier-than-expected obstacle that I needed to take care of before my fast-approaching engagement dinner.

I took a deep breath and pulled the mermaid onto a flat rock, and finally, there was my car. The sun returned behind the clouds, perhaps having seen enough of this. The waves had settled too, no longer poking fun at me.

I pulled the mermaid across the last few feet of gravel and lifted her into the backseat. I then covered her with Sharon's favorite blue dress that I'd picked up from the dry cleaner on my way out of town. Blood soaked through the fabric in the shape of a puffer fish.

Sharon had been wearing that dress when I'd met her at my cousin's wedding, and she'd wanted to wear it for our special dinner tonight. She always talked about how that dress had lured me in, but until I'd dropped it off at the dry cleaner yesterday, I'd been unable to recall it. But I don't really retain things like the clothes we were wearing and what songs the DJ was playing, like Sharon did. I don't even remember the exact moment I met Sharon. We were suddenly together in a group of my old friends at my cousin's wedding, and she tapped me on the shoulder and asked if I'd bring her another drink. She gave me specific instructions of how the drink was to be prepared by the young bartender who was way out of his depth. And I did it. I patiently described each step and vigilantly watched to make sure the bartender did it correctly.

When I returned with her drink, she pressed the glass to

her lips and a smile formed on her stoic face. She drank deeply, her gray eyes never leaving mine, and I felt these little tugs in my chest. Something inside me was trying to reach her. That's what I remember.

That pull from me to her.

"Perfect," Sharon had said. "Perfect." She took my hand, and it felt as if she hadn't let go since.

"I've never been in a metal chariot," the mermaid said as I got into the driver seat. She looked pale but alert.

"You've lost a lot of blood," I said.

"Do you have some stashed somewhere?"

I started the car and pulled onto the freeway. I hit the gas harder than usual, and the mermaid lurched backward with a grunt. I didn't have much time before my engagement dinner. I'd have to drop the mermaid off at the hospital and then somehow slip away to pick her up after I'd popped the question to Sharon. Not to mention that I desperately needed a shower and a new change of clothes. "No, I'll bring you to the doctor."

"Please," she said. "You know I can't go to a doctor. I'm a flipping mermaid. They'll cut me up for science."

I hadn't thought about that. I was so used to her form now that it almost seemed mundane. "Yes, you're right. You're a mermaid."

She touched the blood stain on the dress and winced.

"Is this your dress?" she said. "I've ruined it."

"Not mine. But I think it's supposed to mean a whole lot to me."

"How so?"

I kept my eyes on the road. "Because it means something to my fiancée. Or rather, my girlfriend. But I think you should keep it. I need to make a new memory with Sharon. A shared memory."

"I hate to be picky while bleeding all over your metal chariot, but this dress is not really my style. I prefer a glistening tail and free-floating perky boobs. You've done a remarkable job not staring at them."

"Thank you," I said because it was either a compliment or a trap and the less words spoken about it, the better.

The mermaid politely pulled the dress up to her chin and pressed again on the spot where blood still seeped from her tail.

I thought about how much Sharon loved that dress, and I suddenly felt inordinately sad. Like I'd had one job all these years, and I'd failed. She'd chosen me because I was supposed to tell her when her dresses were ugly. But also when she looked beautiful. And I certainly needed to tell her that I wasn't ready. That I hadn't been ready for any of it.

"I don't know anything about tails," I said, "but maybe we could rip the dress into pieces and use it to tie it off. It could stop the bleeding."

"Sounds good to me."

I parked on the shoulder of the freeway and then leaned over the seat. I reached for the hem of the dress and yanked a strip from the end. The mermaid leaned against the door and pulled up the dress until her wound was exposed. It was deeper than I thought and throbbing slightly with her pulse. I pushed down a wave of nausea as I wrapped the strip around her coarse tail, which was warm and taut and thrumming with energy. Then I tugged it tight.

"Oh, dolphin!" she exclaimed.

"Sorry. Too tight?"

She exhaled loudly with her eyes closed. "No, I think it's good."

"Now what?" I said. "I really want to help you before I go back to my life. I want you to be safe."

She looked out the window. "Take me back to the ocean."

"But what about all that blood? Won't a shark get you?"

"I'd rather take my chances with a shark than your scientists."

"Fair enough," I said. "Think you can swim?"

"I don't know. You mind if I rest here for a few minutes?"

"Take your time," I said. I was still leaning over the seat.

Another slow exhale. "You know. This all started because I was trying to get a better view of two humans kissing on the beach a little way up from you. I could see their entire legs and everything." She smiled and then grimaced. "Sorry. I'm sure that sounded depraved. Hope I didn't freak you out."

"Sharon and I came down this way a few years ago," I said. "Not long after we met. We made out on a beach too. Somewhere around here. We even got in the water. It was a much nicer day than today."

"Is she your girlfriend or your fiancée?"

"I don't know yet."

The mermaid looked me in the eyes, and we both realized it at the same moment. We'd seen each other before. On that day I was with Sharon at the beach.

"I thought you looked familiar," she said.

"You too," I said. "You were watching us."

"Yes. Your lady friend has red hair. And long, lithe legs. The kind that are mesmerizing to watch when she swims."

I'd been putting sunblock on Sharon when I looked up and saw a head poking up from the water. At the time, I thought it was my ex-girlfriend. Like the past was rising up to warn me. I hadn't ended things well with her. In fact, I hadn't ended them at all. I'd been pulled into Sharon's orbit, and I'd let my ex-girlfriend disappear. I hadn't even gone back for my dog. But a second later, the head was gone and with it, my lingering doubts.

"I go up and down the beach watching," the mermaid said. "I've seen so many swimmers over the years. I'm obsessed with legs. The way they alluringly move. Underwater and above water. But you. You were the only one to ever see me. Even for just a second."

"When you were watching," I said, "did you see anything there between Sharon and me? Did you see a spark? Did we seem content? Well-suited? In love?"

"I'm a pervert," the mermaid said, "not some kind of relationship expert."

"Okay, forget I asked," I said. I knew those were things only I could figure out on my own.

That day at the beach, Sharon had actually gone for a swim alone before we'd returned to the car. There was a moment when she dived under a wave and hadn't immediately bobbed to the surface. I'd jumped to my feet, clutching at my clothes. I was ready to jump in after her. But then there she was, the sun glinting off her high cheeks and forehead. She waved to me. At the time it had felt comfortable. But now, thinking back, it felt ominous. A farewell rather than a hello.

"You okay, Screaming Guy?"

I wanted to say yes, that I was fine. That I was preparing for a glorious future with Sharon. "I don't want to get married," I said.

"Me either," she said. "Sounds dreadful."

"I'm proposing to Sharon tonight."

The mermaid looked up at me. "Don't do it. That will solve your problem."

"I have to."

She shrugged. "Well, you make a convincing argument. Did you get her a ring?"

I looked frantically out the back windshield at the endless stretch of road behind us. There was no way I would find the exact spot where I'd been parked. And I knew without a doubt that Sharon's ring was somewhere on those rocks.

"You look more like what I was expecting when I heard you earlier," the mermaid said. "Much more screamy."

"I lost the ring," I said. "Out on the rocks. I was holding it when I went to rescue you."

The mermaid lowered her eyes. "I appreciate you helping me. Even though you did hurt my tail. Let me make it up to you. I'll lead us back to that exact spot."

"You can do that?"

"I'm a flipping mermaid. Of course I can."

I drove until I felt we were in the general vicinity of where we'd met. "This is pretty close," she said. "I'm impressed."

I implored her to put on the dress before I let her climb onto my back. The weight of her, the texture of the dress's fabric against my skin, dislodged a memory from my cousin's wedding. At the end of the night, after my cousin and his wife had disappeared from the dance floor, I'd stumbled on Sharon passed out at a table. Though I was a little unstable myself, I hoisted her into my arms and taken her back to my hotel room. I wasn't sure who she'd come with, but I couldn't leave her there alone. Without touching her dress, I tucked her into my bed and then fell face first onto the couch. The next morning, we got eggs and toast at the buffet.

"This is the beginning of something good," she'd said and smiled.

I had tried to see what she was seeing. I'd been doing it ever since that morning.

The mermaid squeezed my shoulder. "Stop," she said.

I lowered myself onto a rock, and the mermaid slid from my back onto the sand.

"Did you find it?" I said.

She arranged herself into a relaxed posture, her tail coiling out from under Sharon's dress, her shoulders pulled back. "I see it."

I scanned the ground, hoping to catch a glimpse of it too.

"I can get it for you," she said.

But I knew what was more important. "I'll take you to the ocean," I said.

"You don't want the ring?"

"Not like this," I said.

She lifted the dress over her head and spread it across a rock. Then she scooped up a handful of sand and placed it on top. "This will mark the spot."

I picked her up again and stumbled my way to the water.

Once the mermaid was back under the waves, I would drive

to pick up Sharon. Instead of going to dinner, I would bring her back here, where her favorite dress would guide us. Here, with the waves crashing around us, I would tell her everything that was on my mind.

And then, together, we would look for the ring.

Part 3:
No Such Thing As Second Chances

Tale #9: The Lie

Every wave is a water sprite who swims in the current, each current is a path which snakes towards my palace, and my palace is fluidly built at the bottom of the lake, in the triangle of earth, fire, and water.

— attributed to Émile Zola

When I got home from work, Tania was lounging on the couch, watching TV. She waved at me, her arm like a swan's neck, but she didn't get up. When we'd first moved into our apartment, she used to greet me at the door each evening like we were in a black-and-white sitcom from the fifties. I'd call her June because that sounded like one of the moms from those shows, and she'd call me Ward even though I thought it sounded like a guy with erectile dysfunction.

Then Tania's friend at work got pregnant and then Tania's sister and then some lady she saw every day at the coffee shop.

"But you don't even know that lady," I had said, and that's when Tania stopped getting up when I opened the door.

And I stopped calling her June.

"Do you have to be super old to get sciatica?" I asked as I put my bag on the kitchen table.

She didn't turn from the TV. "You getting a new car?"

"No. It's like my ass and the back of my left leg are on fire."

"Fuck," she said. Lately, she'd been dropping f-bombs like a fighter pilot in WWII. "You should get that looked at."

"I'll make an appointment," I said. There was a time when even something as trivial as making an appointment would have been a team effort. Some part of us would be in contact, our knees or elbows, as one of us placed the call. Now she had her back to me watching a TV show that appeared to have a never-ending supply of gunshots, explosions, and quippy one-liners.

I imagined walking over to the couch and kneeling beside her. I'd block her view of the television, but as our eyes met, I'd know I had her full attention. She would feel my attraction for her. She would know how much I'd been missing her. I'd tenderly place two fingertips on her cheek and trace them along her chin. That little whimper noise she used to make would fall involuntarily from her parted lips. I'd give anything to hear her make that sound.

Another explosion from the TV show brought me back to our kitchen, where I stood with my sciatica along with what had become a pretty sizable erection. I didn't want Tania to discover me in this state.

"I'm getting in the shower," I said, which, these days, is where I took care of such matters.

"I bet it will help with the sciatica," she said, a note of care in her voice. "Dull the pain."

I worked with a guy who told me that when he and his wife were trying to have a kid, his wife had all her fertile times marked on the calendar. He claimed that they had sex so much that it stopped being fun. Sex with Tania had never stopped being fun, even during the time when we were desperately trying to get pregnant.

Jerking off in the shower was the thing that had stopped being fun.

Normally, I waited for the shower to get so hot that it completely covered the mirror in steam. I didn't want to accidentally catch a glimpse of me frantically whaling on myself because that would ruin the illusion that Tania had quietly slipped into the shower with me.

I opened the bathroom door and leaned into the hallway. It sounded like there was a lull in the movie.

"I love you," I called to Tania.

"I love you too," she said.

After a year of trying to get pregnant, I had gone to the doctor to test my sperm count. My doctor was a woman, which at first made me feel awkward, but then I realized was perfect. I'd never talked about any sexual encounters with my friends. Nor my feelings. If I wanted to have a frank talk about my inability to get my wife pregnant, this doctor with the bowl-shaped haircut of an elementary school teacher would navigate me through it without feeling stupid.

"Your sperm count is exceptional," she had said. "Elevated, even."

I hadn't been expecting that. I was convinced that my sperm was the problem. That I'd have to take some pills or put ice on my balls or do something to stimulate production. Anything to show Tania how seriously I wanted this baby.

"The next step," she'd said, "is to get your wife to come in."

"I'll talk to her," I'd said. "I'll tell her everything."

#

With the mirror sufficiently covered in steam, I stepped into the shower and closed the glass door. I was about to shut my eyes and hit play on today's fantasy when I heard something in the drain. It gurgled loudly as water tried to navigate some kind of stoppage.

Then something moved, causing the water to gush upward.

A ripple passed along my scalp and neck. A little wave of panic and fear.

"Shit, shit, shit," a voice came from inside the drain.

My brain gave a command to my arm to open the shower door and extract myself from this situation, but nothing happened. I just stood there, staring.

Then a miniature woman pulled herself out of the drain. The shock was so great that I continued to have no reaction. She wore a simple white dress, which had remained completely dry during her trek through the pipes. Her eyes were too large for her face and immensely black. And even as I'd been staring, she'd already begun to imperceptibly grow in size. And then she was hovering in front of me, held aloft by two previously unnoticed shimmering wings, the water from the shower diverting around her.

"Ta-da!" she said.

There was no way I could respond, with my neurons misfiring as they were.

She sighed heavily. "When I was planning this, I pictured myself soaring up from the drain in all my magnificence. I didn't expect for my ass to get stuck in there." She slapped her backside, and the sound was nearly like a slap in the face. I tapped my forehead a few times with my right hand as if to nudge myself back toward sanity.

"I had to rush the reveal, though," she continued, slightly aggravated. "If we're going to be one hundred percent honest with each other, and I think we should, I wanted to catch you before you got started." She pointed at my little dude hanging between my pale, nearly hairless legs.

My initial fear was now fully eclipsed by my embarrassment. I covered myself with both of my hands.

"I wasn't going to do anything," I said.

She wiggled her shoulders with both of her palms face up in front of her, as if weighing which way to respond. "I thought we were going to be one hundred percent honest with each other? We both know what you do in here, and it's no big deal to me. Truly. Though if you want my opinion, I think you do it too much. Like, probably more than is healthy."

"Okay," I said. "I get it. Thank you."

"It's not like you can impregnate black mold."

"Sure, right. Yes. Thank you. Can we please move on?"

She smiled and her black eyes glowed. "Well, now we're both a bit embarrassed. Puts us on equal ground, I guess."

"What are you?" I said.

She looked disappointed. "I thought it was obvious. I'm a water sprite!" She spun in an unsteady circle, her arms awkwardly out to her sides for balance. She bumped against the shampoo shelf hanging from the shower head. "Ta-da," she said again.

"Why are you here?" I said. It was hard to imagine that something magical wanted to have anything to do with me.

"I'm here to help you with your problem."

"My sciatica?"

"No. With your lie."

I knew exactly what lie she was referring to. The only lie that mattered. The lie I told Tania after I went to get my sperm count checked. Because I didn't want Tania to feel disappointed in herself. Ever. I'd rather she felt disappointed in *me*. At the time, I thought I could handle it. That it would be just a tiny bump along the incredibly wonderful road we'd been traveling so far.

I told Tania I had a low sperm count. I researched all the things I could do to keep up the charade. I stopped drinking alcohol. I bought pills that I emptied one at a time into the trash each day. We stuck with the monthly routine until we didn't. I stopped faking pills. Tania stopped marking fertile days on the calendar. And we reached the point where we were at this moment. The moment when a water sprite had sprung from the shower drain.

"Okay," I said. "Let's do it."

The spray of water had grown cold behind the water sprite. She seemed not to notice, but my skin was puckering like a deflated balloon.

"Let's do what?" the water sprite said. Which definitely wasn't what I was expecting her to say.

"You said you were going to help me with my problem."

"Yes. Help. But you're the one that has to come up with the plan."

I thought about Tania on the couch unaware of what was happening in our shower. "I have an idea," I said. "What if I say that my sperm problem is cured?"

"How?"

"Well, I don't know," I said. "A water sprite appeared in the shower and cured me. Then we could reset. She could go to the fertility doctor, finally."

The water sprite shook her head at me, a truly disgusted look on her face. "So a lie got you into this and you want to tell another lie to try to fix it. You couldn't be more of a man if you tried."

"You told me to come up with a plan. I thought this was a safe brainstorming environment. I didn't say every idea I had was going to be gold."

"Clearly."

"I'll just tell her I lied, then," I said with frustration. "About my sperm count."

"Good idea," the water sprite said, an expectant look on her face that was hard to read.

"But if I do that, then what do I need a water sprite for?"

"Because otherwise you'd be trying to impregnate black mold the rest of your life. I'm the catalyst for truth."

At this point, with cold water pooling at my feet, I just wanted to get out and put my clothes on. Maybe sit down.

"I think you broke my drain," I said.

"That's possible," she said. "But when the water stops, my time will be up here. Off to the next guy who needs my help."

It didn't seem like such a bad idea to end this encounter. "If I'm going to come clean to Tania, then can I still ask for something magical from you? Regarding my sciatica?"

"God, it's always about you. Look. The main reason Tania is trying to *fix* your sperm," the water sprite said, with the word "fix" in air quotes, "is so that you forgive yourself. That you stop being so hard on yourself. It's not about a baby. It's about you. She's worried about you."

"You've talked to Tania?" I said.

"Yeah, why do you think I'm here? Did you think I was just randomly feeling sorry for you? In the end, no matter what Tania says, you really are just a man, aren't you? A regular, self-absorbed man."

I didn't think that was entirely fair, but I didn't want to continue arguing with a water sprite about all my deficiencies. I wanted to keep us on subject. "How did Tania know how to contact you?"

"I don't know," the water sprite said. "Maybe she checked out a book at the library?"

Something coursed through me. It had been a while, but I'd describe it as hope. "So this all started because I was worried about Tania's feelings, and now she's worried about mine?"

The water sprite threw her arms up in mock delight. "What a love story!"

"Do you know if she still wants to have a baby?" Because it suddenly occurred to me that it probably wasn't me who needed a water sprite. And if I came clean, Tania would realize it too.

"I have no idea," the water sprite said. "I can't read minds!"

"I'm going to turn off the water now," I said. Seemed polite to give her a heads up.

She shrugged. "I'm going to be one hundred percent honest one last time. Don't nibble Tania's ear. She hates that."

"She told you that?"

"I told you I couldn't read minds."

I turned off the water.

I wrapped myself in a towel and went into the bedroom to put on a pair of sweatpants. I was surprised to find Tania lying in bed, reading.

"How was the movie?" I said.

93

"It was fine. A little loud, I guess. I wanted something quiet." She smiled at me.

The air crackled with possibility. Perhaps the only magic the water sprite had performed was to keep me from masturbating in the shower. I wanted to follow where this went.

"You seem flushed or something," Tania said.

"I'm fine. Let me get ready, and I'll join you."

I grabbed my sweatpants and a T-shirt and escaped to the bathroom. My heart was racing. I was nervous. Extremely nervous.

I put on my clothes and brushed my teeth. The water in the shower hadn't completely drained yet, and I could see my terrified reflection on its surface. I was going to have to call a plumber for sure.

"What's going on in there?" Tania called from our bedroom. Expectant.

"Something wrong with the drain."

"Forget about it and come back here."

I was resolved to tell her about the lie in that instant. She would understand why I'd done it. And we could set it right. We could be in constant contact again.

Tania put her book on the side table when I returned to the bedroom and patted the spot next to her.

"Something happened in the shower?" she said. Her eyes sparkled.

"I don't know," I said, unsure of myself now. "Water won't drain."

"Oh," she said. Disappointed. I knew why, of course. She was waiting for a water sprite to appear. The water sprite she had summoned. And afterward, everything would be fixed.

But suddenly I felt incredibly stupid. Like I'd wasted my allotted time with a magical creature. And I had no idea how hard it had been for Tania to put her plan into motion. What had she given of herself to conjure a water sprite? I mean, it seemed impossible. She had somehow changed the fabric of everyday reality. I couldn't let her know how badly I'd bungled my one opportunity. Because the answer was obvious to me now. I had to take myself out of the equation. The way forward was to have the water sprite visit Tania. So I was going to find her again. I'd be ready the next time. I could still set everything right.

"Nothing happened in there?" Tania asked.

"Just the normal stuff," I said. "Shampoo, soap, rinse."

She turned away from me, her head on the pillow. "We'll call a plumber."

"Of course," I said. "Tomorrow."

I lay down next to her. I could feel her breathing. Her back rising and falling as if searching for me. I rolled to my side and pressed my face into the lustrous wonder of her hair.

Then, as I pivoted to put my arm around her and pull her closer to me, an electric stab of pain shot down my left leg.

I rolled away from her, the pain ebbing as I tried to remember the name of the plumber we had called last time a pipe had burst in the kitchen. It seemed like a very long time ago. Tania would remember his name, I was certain, but I couldn't ask her.

I left the space between us.

Tale #10: Classified

Where there's a labyrinth, there's a minotaur, and vice versa!
I can't imagine a decent maze that would be caught dead
without a minotaur.

— Catherynne M. Valente,
The Girl Who Fell Beneath Fairyland and Led the Revels There

Haley and I had been broken up for two weeks when she asked
if I'd drive up north to have dinner with her parents.

"They are looking forward to meeting you," she said over
the phone, and I could picture the wince that happened when
she felt uncomfortable. The twitch of her cheek.

"Won't they think it's weird we aren't together anymore?"
I said.

"Not if we don't tell them," she said. "I thought about
getting someone to pretend to be you, but my parents would
never buy it. And you know me so well already."

But that was the thing; I didn't really know her. It was
pretty much why we broke up. During our few months
together, we'd talked only about the present moment, our
shared experiences, as if she'd materialized out of the ether to
go to movies with me, eat at my favorite restaurants, and peri-
odically leave her bras at my apartment. We'd had a nice time,

a better than nice time, even, but if I ever asked her about her life outside our bubble, she would joke that it was "classified" or "complicated." I found her inscrutability to be torture, and I'd plagued myself with thoughts of her other life, her other loves, her other selves.

In fact, I'd actually done the breaking up part for the first time in my life. It was bizarre. I did such a poor job of it that when I dropped Haley off at her apartment building after a meal spent discussing the merits of tapioca balls in tea, she asked me if we were over.

"Yes," I'd said.

Which was the same exact thing I said in response to meeting her parents. Because maybe Haley had spent the last two weeks thinking about me, too. Maybe she had dreamed up this whole dinner with her parents to show me she was willing to start sharing. Maybe she was ready to trust me.

#

It turned out that it wasn't just dinner; it was a weekend at her parent's house. The actual house where Haley had grown up. It was away from the lights of the city and near a lake, and I hoped it was full of family pictures. I wanted to see what had come before we met.

"Just so you know, they would never let us stay in the same room," she said as we drove out of the city in her little two-door sedan. "So it won't be awkward or anything. You know, having to sleep in the same bed."

"It wouldn't have been awkward."

Something flared in the air between us, like charged ozone. I knew if it were ignited, I'd surely never let her out of my sight again.

"So why the ruse?" I asked. "And don't say it's classified."

"If you want to know the truth, Mom is dying. And I want her to see I'm happy before she goes."

My tongue clicked against the roof of my mouth. The wheels of the car whooshed along the road like whispering mourners at a funeral. I had no idea what to say.

Haley tilted the rearview mirror toward me, and when our eyes met, she laughed loudly. A big sound that came from somewhere deep inside her. "Oh my god. I'm sorry. I was just kidding. I couldn't even keep a straight face when I said it."

"Looked pretty straight to me," I said.

"Oh, you're angry at me now." She pushed out her lower lip.

"I'm not angry. It's just, how would I know you weren't telling the truth? I know nothing about you."

"You know what I look like naked."

I couldn't help it. I blushed. I was no prude in the bedroom, but any frank discussion of sex while fully clothed sent the blood rushing to my head like a schoolgirl.

"But please don't tell my parents you know that," Haley said.

#

By the time we got to her parents' house, I couldn't tell if we were back together. And it wasn't until we were driving up the long driveway, hemmed in on both sides by hulking trees, that I realized she'd never told me why we were deceiving her parents. The rust-colored brick house itself was modest, although quite beautiful.

"That's my room up there," Haley said as she stopped under a car port. She pointed up at the corner window. The light was on, and I thought I saw the shadow of someone standing inside. "Mom's probably making the bed now."

The shadow turned, and in the second before the light turned out, I thought I saw a snout and two curved horns on its head.

Haley slugged me on the arm. "You okay?"

"Yeah, I'm looking forward to meeting your mom," I said. "I'm really glad she's not dying."

"But aren't we all dying?"

"I prefer to push that out of my mind."

"Oh, hey," Haley said, slapping my knee. "I forgot to tell you. The house is old and it settles in weird ways. It sometimes moans at night."

"Moans?"

"You get used to it."

"Moans?" I said again. "Can't you pick another less creepy word?"

"Whatever you do, don't try to figure it out. Dad hates when guys think they know more than him. Plus you'll just get lost in the house. You aren't going to win him over by fixing it."

"Oh, I'm trying to win him over?"

"Aren't you?"

As she popped the trunk and got out, I realized that was the first bit of information about her life she'd ever told me.

#

I grabbed both of our bags and followed Haley up to the door. Before we'd entered the arc of the porchlight, the door flung open and a burly man ran out, his arms opening wide as he ran toward us. It was disconcerting. With the shadows dancing around, I couldn't tell if he was happy to see us or if he was planning to mow us down. But a moment later he had Haley in a crushing hug, and she laughed as she thrashed at his completely bald head.

"Haley Bear!" he roared.

"Put me down, Dad!"

He did as he was told and then turned his expansive face to me. I took a step back, unaccustomed to such open displays of affection. My parents barely acknowledged they'd spawned me if more than two people were in the room.

"Not a hugger?" Haley's dad said with an impish grin.

"Well, I don't know, I wouldn't say that," I said, not wanting to disappoint Haley.

"Good," he said, and then he pounced. I felt his arms around my biceps before I even saw him move. He smelled like cinnamon, and heat barreled from his hairless face like gamma rays. The bags fell heavily to the ground at my feet.

"You're crushing him!" Haley said, still laughing.

And indeed he was. I had stopped attempting to breathe and was apparently awaiting the slow embrace of death.

Haley's dad let go, and I realized he'd lifted me completely off the ground. My knees buckled as my feet reconnected with the earth, and I barely kept myself upright.

Haley and her dad laughed identical laughs as I sucked in air and waited for the stars to stop popping in my vision.

"So, this is the guy, huh?" Haley's dad said.

"That's the one," Haley said.

I coughed.

#

In the light of the house, Haley's dad was much older than I'd originally thought. He had to be at least seventy years old, but everything about him was taut and coiled and vibrating with energy. Haley's mother was a good twenty years younger. She wore her dark hair in a bun and had perfectly erect posture. She looked demure and a little humorless.

"I keep myself virile for this wildcat here," Haley's dad said as Haley's mom lit a candle on the table already set with food. When he pounded both fists on his chest, it sounded like a boulder striking the side of a barge.

"Nobody wants to hear you talk that way," Haley's mom said. "Now, let's eat."

Haley pulled me to the table without introducing me to her mom. I had no idea how I was supposed to address either of them, which was giving me a fair bit of anxiety. I certainly couldn't call them Mom and Dad.

But I shouldn't have worried, because no one really talked. After such a warm reception, I was surprised at the lack of conversation. They focused on the chicken and green beans and apple cobbler as if it were all going to disappear if any of them looked away.

"This is delicious," I said.

"Of course it is," Haley's dad said. "My wife made it."

And that was it.

#

Haley's mom walked us upstairs after she'd cleared all the plates from the table. I'd looked in the entranceway and along the hallways and had yet to see a picture. I needed that glimpse of the past. I had this nagging sensation that Haley and I weren't the only ones pretending things were different than they were.

"I put him in the office," Haley's mom said, as if both Haley and I weren't standing there. "There's the pullout couch."

"Thank you," I said.

She didn't look at me. Haley opened the door and ushered me in.

"You're across the hall," her mom said to her.

"I know where my room is, Mom. I'm going to get him settled."

"All right. But no horseplay."

"Promise," Haley said as if this was completely normal.

The office was small. It barely had enough room for the wooden desk and the cracked leather couch.

"I wanted you to know that there isn't enough room to pull out the couch," said Haley. "No one has ever told Mom, so we let her keep on believing there is. You mind sleeping on the couch itself?"

"I don't mind, it looks comfortable enough," I said. "But I don't understand. Why not tell her?"

"It works better this way." Haley put a stack of sheets and a pillow on the couch. "I hope you're able to sleep."

Haley moved to the door, and I grasped her hand, not wanting her to leave yet.

"I can't stay," she said.

"Why did your parents want to meet me? They barely spoke to me. I mean, they barely spoke at all."

"What did you want them to say?"

"I don't know. Ask me about myself or something."

"I told them all about you," she said.

"Like what?"

Haley smiled. "Everything. Sleep tight!"

#

The couch wasn't comfortable. I tried putting my head at both ends. I tried with a pillow and without. I tried wrapping the whole couch in a sheet. It wasn't going to happen. So I gave up and walked over to the desk. I thought I'd find something personal inside, but that thought was immediately dashed. The two drawers were empty, and there wasn't a single piece of paper on the surface. Or a picture frame. Whoever used this as an office wasn't really using it. I wished I'd brought a book because there wasn't a single thing to occupy my mind.

Then came the moan.

All the hair on my neck stood on end. It was not the moan of a house settling. It was the moan of a creature in trouble.

It was the moan of despair.

Then it came again. No longer only lugubrious, it now had the distinct whiff of fear. Whatever was making the sound needed help.

I clicked open the door to the dark hallway. Haley and her family seemed unconcerned. Everything was as silent as our meal. There was literally no way I could ever get used to that moaning sound.

Something huffed at the end of the hallway. Almost like a horse.

"Hello?" I said.

"Go back to bed," came a quivering voice from the shadows.

"It's a couch, actually," I said, hoping to diffuse some tension.

"Shove your semantics up your arse."

I stepped back into the office. "Will do. I'll get right on it."

As soon as I shut the door, I heard the moan again, so close now that it was like fingers tapping directly on my spine.

Thump. Thump. Thump. Like hooves passing my room.

"You're an idiot," I muttered to myself as I slowly opened the door and peered into the hallway.

A hulking man was passing. All I saw was his T-shirt that said WHAT ARE YOU LOOKING AT? and a pair of cut-off jean shorts before he was out of my line of sight.

I counted to ten and then stepped out of the office quickly before I lost my nerve. There waiting for me was a man with a bull's head on top of his shoulders. His big bull nostrils flared, and his dewy bull eyes were fixed on me. His horns, curled over his head, looked moist in the dim light.

Somehow I didn't try to run or scream or squeeze my eyes shut, all of which I wanted to do. Desperately.

The bull man huffed.

"I expected someone bigger. And more attractive," he said.

I nodded. That sounded about right.

"But I'm definitely surprised you walked out here. Haley said you would, but most people let you down. So tell me, why'd you step into the hall?" When the bull man talked, his mouth moved, but it was unclear how he was forming words.

"You're staring at my mouth," he said.

"No," I said. "I'm sorry. I mean, I am. Staring at your mouth. But I'll stop. Please don't kill me."

"I'm not going to kill you!" he roared. "Way to rush to judgment based on my looks. For all I know, you're one of those big game hunters with endangered animals mounted on your wall, but you don't see me assuming that."

"Yes," I said rather lamely.

"So are you?"

"What?"

"A big game hunter?"

"Oh no. I've never killed anything."

"Well, me either."

But then he smiled, and it was a very scary thing to behold. I looked away from his face and down to his bulging biceps and his overly hairy legs. There was even a tail I hadn't noticed before, flicking silently in the dark.

"You didn't answer me," he said. "Why are you here?"

I thought about Haley and how vulnerable I felt in our relationship. "I wanted to know more about Haley. Like maybe we'd bond over childhood experiences. I hoped meeting her parents and seeing her childhood home would help us. But I don't even know their names. And we barely spoke at all. I had so many questions."

The bull man snorted. "You can't expect people you just met to tell you their life story. You have to earn that. So, is that why you're here? You ready to earn it?"

As scary as this creature was, I felt compelled to listen to him. He seemed to have the answers I was looking for. "Yes. That's why I'm here."

"Okay then, follow me."

"Follow you?"

"Unless you want to go back to your couch and tug your man bits or something."

"No, I'm cool. Let's go."

"And you can address me as The Minotaur."

"With the 'the' included?" I asked.

"Of course."

It wasn't until we were on the stairs that I realized I was in my boxers and a T-shirt and barefoot. "Sorry to bother you,

The Minotaur, but where are we going?"

"Do you have to know the reason for everything before you make a move? You can't always prepare for the future, man. Sometimes you follow a minotaur against your better judgment wearing only your jammies."

"Oh." I faltered. "Is this against my better judgment?"

"You're the one who broke up with Haley," he huffed and stomped down the stairs.

"But not because I didn't like her."

"We'll see about that."

I followed after him, my toes cold in the night air. The floor creaked as I stepped onto another landing, another hallway. I didn't remember going up two flights of stairs after dinner.

"The Minotaur?" I said. But he was gone.

There was another set of stairs going down and two doors at the end of the hall. He must have continued down the stairs. I took them two at a time, hoping to catch him, but found myself alone again in an identical hallway. I ran back up the stairs only to find the same hallway again. I was caught in some kind of loop.

Then there was the moaning again, somewhere very far away now. I ran to the end of the hall and tried both of the doors. Locked. I was losing at my attempts not to panic, so I sat down right there on the carpet.

After a few minutes of deep breathing and making sure my balls didn't slip out of my boxers, I slowly got to my feet. If I went up one more flight of stairs, I'd be back at the office. By not panicking, maybe I could at least get back to where I'd started. I really wanted to talk to Haley. I wanted to ask her what this all meant. Was The Minotaur the key to our possible future?

Something shuffled on the stairs below, and I saw the flicker of a light. A moment later, there was Haley's mom, holding a candle on a plate like she was in a Victorian novel.

"You've decided to do it," she said, and she actually looked pleased. It was the first time she'd spoken to me directly.

"Do what?"

"Challenge The Minotaur."

I didn't like the sound of that. "In what way?"

"In a challenging way."

"Like a game of chess? Or Scrabble? Or a rap battle?"

Haley's mom looked less pleased.

"I don't know what's going on," I said.

"Surely you've heard of minotaurs and mazes and all that? Our house is a maze. But only at night. Makes going for a snack at midnight a nuisance, but you get used to it." She patted the pocket of her nightgown, and I saw an enormous piece of brownie wedged in there.

"How do you get back?"

"There's a series of patterns. Like for you, to get to the minotaur's lair, you just go up, up, down, down, left, right, left, right, B, A. Then select and start."

"Starting from where?"

"Anywhere. As you already know, you can't get back to the office the way you came."

"Wait. So there's a different pattern to get me back to the office?"

"Of course there is, but do you want it?"

Did I? I thought of Haley's tilted smile that caused her right eye to close just enough to seem like a wink. My leg still tingled from when she'd slugged me earlier in the car. Maybe I would challenge The Minotaur if it meant that Haley and I could connect on a deeper level.

"Well, that's as close to a no as we're likely to get," Haley's mom said.

"I don't understand the B and the A and the rest."

"You'll figure it out."

"Hold on. Has anyone challenged The Minotaur before?" I tried to imagine Haley's previous boyfriends in the same predicament I was finding myself in.

"Yes."

"How did it go?"

"Not that well, I hate to say." She peered at me over her candle. "But you surprise me. I didn't think much of you when you arrived. But here you are, on your way to the lair. I can see a little bit of the good things Haley said about you. Your steadfastness. Your determination. And with such kindness."

"She said those things about me?"

Haley's mom shook her head. "Have more confidence," she said. "And with that, I must say goodnight."

If I wanted to get back, all I needed to do was follow her. She moved to the adjacent stairwell.

"That couch doesn't pull out," I said. If Haley had told her some things about me, then I could tell her something she didn't already know. Something she needed to know.

She cocked her head to the side. "What do you mean?"

"The room isn't big enough. To accommodate it."

"That's simply not true."

"I'm afraid it is."

Even though I'd managed to keep her standing there, I still didn't know what to do.

"Well, thanks for letting me know," she said.

"What should I call you?" I said. "Haley never properly introduced us."

"Let's wait and see how you do with The Minotaur," she said. "People come out different than when they went in."

Before I could say anything else, she slipped up the stairs and out of sight.

With no way of getting back to Haley, I decided to try the pattern. I went up again, stopping to check if I'd returned to the office. I had not, just as Haley's mom had said. So, it was up another flight according to the pattern. Then down twice. I was actually working up quite a sweat. I went left and right in order both times, curving down hallways that I hadn't seen before, and that's when I finally found a small alcove that was different. Two doors, one with marked with an A and one with a B. I stepped through B and found myself in the same room with the same choices.

But also Haley's dad was now there too.

"There he is!" he bellowed. "I knew you were made of sterner stuff."

"What exactly gave you that impression?" I said.

"Just a hunch."

"But we barely spoke at dinner."

Haley's dad shrugged. "No one wanted to get attached yet."

I took a deep breath, very sure of myself. "I can't beat a minotaur."

Haley's dad guffawed. "You mean The Minotaur? Not with that attitude, you won't."

"I don't understand why you'd all send me to my death. You don't even know me."

"That's rubbish. Nobody is going to die. You just have to prove your mettle."

I stood there staring at him with no idea what to believe.

"Now take off your shirt," he said.

I was too numb now to argue. I pulled off my shirt without hesitation and dropped it next to me.

Haley's dad stared at me, a little puzzled. "Your chest is concave."

"Yeah, like I said, I don't think I'll instill much fear in The Minotaur."

"Likely not. But I still have high hopes."

"That makes one of us."

I wished Haley were here right now. If only I could see her, maybe ask her a few questions, this whole thing would be easier. I still wasn't entirely sure what I was fighting for.

"You're almost there. Go through that door marked A. Choose your weapon."

"Weapon?"

"Oh, and one last thing. You have to be completely nude

before you challenge The Minotaur."

The room on the other side of the A door looked medie-
val. Racks of gleaming weapons. Axes and maces and swords
and whips and shields and some stuff I'd never seen before.
Every single one looked like the kind of thing people died
while holding.

At either end of the room was a door. One said EXIT and
was bolted with a rusty padlock. The other said START in
bright red letters. I scanned the racks, looking for the smallest
weapon, something I was least likely to hurt myself with as I
attempted to wield it. Then I thought *screw it* and grabbed the
biggest shield. My focus was definitely on protecting myself.
It was too heavy to hold aloft, so I had to push it along the
carpet toward the door marked START.

It was slightly ajar, just enough to see movement but not
enough to tell who, or what, was inside. I tugged the waist of
my boxers, not wanting to pull them off. It was really bothering me that The Minotaur might be naked too. Chances were
high that he'd be hung like a bull. And there I'd be with my
skinny arms and paunchy belly.

I moved closer. Voices.

"Do you think he'll fight?" said The Minotaur.

"He's uncertain sometimes. A little self-conscious. Which
I find kind of adorable." That voice was Haley. The subject was
me, of course. "But when he sets his mind to something, he
won't stop until he's done. He wants to know me better, but
it wasn't until we broke up that I realized I wanted to keep
getting to know him, too. I didn't tell him I had a minotaur
guarding all my secrets. That he'd have to stand up to you. But
he came out of the office. He followed you. Mom gave him the
route. He's going to fight."

"Do you actually want him to fight? He won't win, Haley."

"He would if you let him."

"Well then," The Minotaur said. "Do you want him to
win?"

Haley hesitated.

In that silence, there would be plenty of time to pull off my boxers and lift the shield in front of me. I could push through the door, and neither of them would be able to see me. Maybe instead of confronting The Minotaur, I could get Haley to come with me. Away from this house. From the maze of the past. From a minotaur who guarded all her secrets.

And from behind the shield, I could keep everything about me hidden.

Tale #11: Luck

I have keen eyes. I once caught a leprechaun, you know.

— Brandon Sanderson, *Steelheart*

I was sitting on my back porch, staring at the near-perfect ring stained into the wood, one of the only signs that Tammy had once been here with her fifty-pound, Southwestern-themed planter that seemed to exist solely to catch rainwater, when Bosco bounded up from the fence carrying a dead leprechaun in his mouth.

"Drop it!" I yelled, and Bosco did as he was told, somehow retaining all the commands he had learned in a dog training course Tammy and I had taken him to five years ago.

The leprechaun hit the ground with a thud, and Bosco ran off to continue exploring, his white fur puffing out like a dandelion refusing to release its seeds.

I knelt next to the little man who was no longer than the distance from my wrist to my elbow. As one would imagine, he was dressed in a dark green suit, and rather miraculously, he still had a black hat atop his wispy red hair. His face was ruddy, as if he'd had a distillery somewhere in my backyard, with a tiny curved nose and slightly upturned mouth that never allowed him to stop smiling, even in death.

I remembered when Tammy had moved in with me from across town. It had been raining all morning, but when we'd finally finished getting everything out of her apartment, including that Southwestern-themed pot, the rain had stopped and a rainbow had stretched across the sky.

"It looks like it ends in our yard," she said, even though we couldn't see my house from there, with the freeway and the mall and the new housing developments in the way. But I'd liked the way she'd said *our yard*.

Like most sane people, I'd never believed in leprechauns. But there he lay, proof that maybe Tammy had been right, right about everything. I gingerly plucked him from the grass. He had more heft than I expected from a magical creature, as if my inability to believe in him would cause him to weigh nothing at all. I placed him delicately next to the ring stain on the porch and returned to my chair. It had been a few weeks, but I still couldn't believe Tammy had left this one cushioned deck chair for me. Like she knew exactly where I'd need to be after she was gone.

I looked down at the leprechaun, everything about him impeccable. Not a smudge of dirt. Not a hair out of place. No sign of having spent any time in Bosco's mouth. I wondered what Tammy would see if she were here instead of in her new apartment with a few of my things she'd taken with her. Perhaps she'd notice something out of place, some sign of what had brought about his untimely demise. But from my point of view, it seemed impossible that the leprechaun could be dead.

In the two years we'd lived together, I'd never once convinced Tammy to sit outside with me. "I have to keep moving or I might never move again," she'd said in explanation. I hadn't understood it at the time, but now I pictured her fluttering around somewhere as far away from my chair and the ring-stained porch as she could get, forever outside my orbit. A brand new life that no longer included me.

Bosco barked gleefully from the fence, calling me over to

him. *Hurry up! Hurry up!* he was saying. I rose from the chair and shuffled out into the yard, going past the grill for the first time in over a year. Maybe there was a pot of gold out there.

But I doubted it.

Tale #12: Court of Common Pleas

Humbaba's mouth is fire; his roar the floodwater;
his breath is death. Enlil made him guardian
of the Cedar Forest, to frighten off the mortal
who would venture there. But who would venture
there?

— The Epic of Gilgamesh, Tablet II

While Sarah was out of town, my son and I had to do the grocery shopping ourselves. I was supposed to buy copious amounts of fresh vegetables because Sarah thought neither our son nor I ate enough of them. My plan had been to impress her with our vegetable consumption while she was away. Instead, I cheated on her.

In fact, I'd cheated on Sarah early in our relationship. Before we'd bought a house. Before our son. We'd never talked about it, but I was pretty sure she knew. It didn't seem like anything I'd ever do again, so I'd eliminated it from our possible futures.

My son and I ran into Carla at the supermarket, of course. The exact place Sarah told us to go while she was away. Carla used to date a friend of mine in high school, and I'd always had a thing for her. She still had the same shaggy hair and faded clothes and downturned mouth. In the fluorescent lights of the produce section, she was like a prism refracting new possibilities. We flirted, right next to the vegetables I didn't end up buying, in a way that I didn't know I was capable of while my son clutched my leg with both hands. It was kind of exhilarating. But I should have left it there. A quick adrenaline spike. I shouldn't have accepted her offer for my son and me to come over. She claimed she had some pictures from the old days when she and I were in high school. Before mobile phones and social media. Her husband and children were out of town, so Carla let my son play her son's PlayStation while she and I went into her room and did the thing that people do when they cheat on their spouses.

We both regretted it. We said we'd never contact each other again.

Unfortunately, I never got to see her pictures of me when I was young and perfect and not a total mess. When I hadn't yet become someone who cheats. When I still thought I was going to turn out amazing. I would have liked to see that version of me again.

My son and I continued with our day and never talked about it. We got ice cream and went to the movies and then we ordered pizza for a late dinner, and I thought I'd buried the experience with better experiences.

Then the next day, he told Sarah all about it over the phone while I sat there listening, pretending that everything he was saying wasn't bothering me. At one point he looked at me, and I even gave him a thumbs up. When they were done talking, Sarah asked me not to be there when she got home.

"My mom will come to the house at 11 a.m. on the day I am due to return," Sarah said. "She will not say a word to you. She will not make eye contact. Have a bag packed and walk out. Don't come back." We both breathed into the void separating us.

"I'm getting a dragon." She said it exactly the same way as the woman in the TV commercial who said she got a dragon because her husband had cheated on her, and she was pleased to discover it happened to be 20 percent off in honor of Valentine's Day. That was it. Sarah wanted to keep me away from her so badly she was willing to pay an exorbitant price to have an immensely huge fire-breathing creature block me from returning to our home.

It was going to be insanely hard to win her back.

I didn't tell my son things had gotten pretty fucked because of his choice of topic during his conversation with his mom. He was only seven, but he was so smart that it made me doubt my role in his creation. We had two more nights to spend together. I let him stay up as late as he wanted. I played any video game he suggested. We ate ice cream out of the pint. It was the most fun I'd had in years.

And then I did exactly what Sarah told me to do.

#

Over the next few days, I saw dragons everywhere, perched on houses wherever I went. Normally, in the course of my regular life, before I'd gone to Carla's house, I had ignored them. They were someone else's bad luck. They didn't have anything to do with me. But now each one was a reminder that I had ruined not just my life, but also the lives of two people I cared for deeply.

There was even a nasty looking one outside the window of my hotel. It was huddled on top of a two-story home, its tail flicking across the fence line. It yawned once, and fire danced in its throat. I stopped opening my curtains.

I couldn't believe that this version of me sitting in a dark hotel room crying into washcloths that smelled like ancient lube was in the same timeline as the guy who'd been okay going home with Carla. I was unable to recall how I justified it. How I went through with it. That guy in the supermarket with his son clutching his legs, desperate to pull his father out of the situation, was as indecipherable to me as a government form.

I have always thought about life in terms of timelines. Every decision you made created a new path. No matter how big or small. There are millions of versions of me extending into the cosmos. Branching and splitting over a decision whether to eat potato chips or choosing between two movies. From my point of view, every possible outcome is played fully to the end. How was life after I decided to eat those potato chips? Did anything change after I chose the horror movie over the comedy? Decisions are easier to make when you know that every possible variation will eventually occur.

There's a timeline where my son and I didn't go to Carla's house. The two of us probably bought vegetables and attempted to eat them all. Then, when Sarah returned home, we all cuddled together on the couch and let Sarah choose the movie. But in the timeline where I now found myself, I'd been outcast. I had to figure out if there was a way to jump from where I was, to where I wanted to be. In a quantum sense. Could I leave this timeline and return to another?

The answer, of course, was: not a damn chance. The only way forward was through a dragon.

#

There were many tales of people who had made their way past a dragon to be reunited with the person they had wronged. They probably lived happily ever after. The rest were piles of ash on the sidewalk. You could sometimes see a dragon taking to the sky after successfully dispatching the object of his very expensive ire. Hiring a dragon could sometimes signify finality. In this case, when a dragon was hired, the one being targeted went about his sad little existence and never came back. But in other cases, the dragon could signify that there was still a chance. That all you had to do with your balding, doughy, middle-aged body was get past a fire-breathing dragon and, maybe, you would be forgiven.

Otherwise, it was the ash on the sidewalk option.

I decided in my completely dark hotel room that the quiet little life we'd built was worth fighting for. I put on the shirt Sarah had bought me for Christmas that seemed a little out of season with its red-and-green color palette, along with the necklace my son had made for me out of shell-shaped pasta noodles, and I returned to our home. I still thought of it as our home. A home we could continue to make together. A home where I had changed the timbre and the resonance, but I was going to set it right.

But holy shit, the dragon Sarah rented was intimidating even from the freeway. And it was the only one in our whole neighborhood. He cradled our house like an egg, his wings settled on the ground but still bristling with energy. His mean little eyes scanned the street, and smoke puffed from his nose.

I parked at the end of the block, hoping that the walk would give me a little more time to feel brave. I'd heard the trick to getting past a dragon was to hide your fear. But he recognized me before I got to our driveway.

"Halt," the dragon said in a booming voice. His claws gripped the roof in the exact spot where Sarah and I had sat drinking wine on the night we'd moved in. We'd climbed out of our bedroom window and lay there watching the stars and the occasional dragon soaring past. We hadn't talked or congratulated ourselves on buying a house or anything. We'd just sat there, experiencing it together. It was sort of wonderful.

The green dragon craned his reptilian head down to me and sniffed the air. Then something that sounded like a laugh belched out of him with a plume of smoke.

"Oh wow, peasant," he said finally. "Mistress Sarah thought you might show up, but I didn't believe it. Did you not see me up here?"

"I saw you," I said, but my words were nothing compared to the weight of the dragon.

"My orders are to turn you into a pitiful pile of ash the

moment you step into the yard. Then Mistress Sarah wants to sweep you up and mail you to Mistress Carla with a note that says: 'He's all yours.'"

I knew this was the way it worked, but it hurt to hear aloud. That Sarah had chosen the burning death option for me. But I was already burning on the inside with remorse and self-hatred and, actually, who fucking cares? No one was going to feel sorry for me after what I did. No one was going to take pity. Maybe I wouldn't even feel the dragon's fire.

"We have a son," I said. "We have a history." I stepped onto the curb.

"From what I gather, peasant, you forgot both of those things in the moment, didn't you? And I wouldn't come any closer if I were you."

"Yes," I said. "I sometimes only think about myself. It's true. I see myself as a good person, but I'm not actually always a good person. And I ignore those things about me. But I don't want to do that anymore."

"Lucky you! Because those things are hard to do when you are dead." The dragon laughed again.

Tears had bivouacked behind my eyeballs. I wanted to cry so badly like I'd done all those days and nights alone in the hotel room. But I wasn't here to get sympathy. This time, right here on the curb in front of my house, I wanted to cry with anger. I was shaking with it. I wanted to cry for Sarah and my son and everything we'd lost that we'd never get back.

"Can you pass along a message for me?" I said.

"Fuck no. I'm not your steward. This is the Court of Common Pleas. I will hear you out, but I will not let you pass."

"I don't know what to do."

"Leave. Don't come back. It's incredibly easy, peasant."

"It doesn't feel right," I said. "To go forward without my family."

"Doesn't feel right, does it?" Fire jumped from his nostrils. "You don't get to decide what feels right anymore."

Then the door opened and there was my son. A huge grin on his face.

"Dad! How cool is Tony?"

I didn't think Tony was cool at all.

"Not as cool as you," the dragon said to my son.

My son had a magical way of bringing people, and I guess murderous lizards, together.

"Mom said he was all your fault."

"Are you thanking me?" I said. I looked up at the dragon and tried to see him as my son saw him. He was quite majestic. I'd never been this close to one before.

I grinned at my son, and he grinned back at me. Then he ran across the yard to give me a hug. It felt so good to have him in my arms. We had always spent a lot of time together, but we rarely embraced like that. I vowed to do it more in whatever time I had left.

The dragon stared at us with his dark eyes, and I thought I saw my son and me reflected in there. With my son in my arms, I realized maybe this would be all the time I had left. That this was the last hug. Which was why I didn't want to let go.

"I miss you," I said.

"Why don't you come home?"

"Tony is going to kill me if I come one step closer."

My son pulled away from me and shook his head. "No, he isn't."

"I'm afraid I will, my little knight," breathed the dragon. But I sensed something I hadn't noticed before. A small hesitation. Like maybe there was a chance.

"I'll talk to him," my son said. "I don't think Tony could actually kill someone."

"I've killed a lot of people," the dragon said. "Sorry to disappoint you, but I quite enjoy it."

"Let's not push our luck," I said. "Did your mom say anything?"

My son nodded. "Oh, right. She said she still loves you, but she never wants to see you again."

"Even if I get past the dragon?"

"Dad. You can't get past the dragon."

It stung somewhere deep inside me that he didn't believe I could do it. But then he took my hand in both of his and said, "Not without our help."

I liked the sound of that.

My son turned and ran back into the house.

"You're a decent dad," the dragon said. "Not the best or anything. I wouldn't get it on a mug. But decent. It's too bad you're going to be dead soon."

"Sarah still loves me."

"Of course she does." The dragon shook his head. "If she didn't, she wouldn't bother hiring me and she wouldn't spend any time wishing ill upon you."

"That makes sense," I said.

I thought about dying. How the only thing tethering me to this world were the things I felt were unfinished. Perhaps when I was younger, it didn't seem so bad to die one day in the future. It was abstract. And there was a lot of shit to do before then. But now, dying felt like abandonment. I'd be leaving my son behind without a dad. I'd be leaving Sarah with no answers. No closure. The pointlessness of it all overwhelmed me. Did it matter if I cheated? I believed, very strongly, that it did. But why? Why did it matter? It wasn't the meaning of life I was after. It was the why. Because after I died, there would be no answer to the question of why I had been here at all. The universe would swallow me up, and then in the blink of an eye, everyone else would be swallowed up too. And then the world would end for me. And I would be inconsequential in all that had come to pass.

The dragon studied me, its massive wings shuttering. "I see a look in your eye. Like you're planning to take a step forward. If you think I'm not going to incinerate you because you're brave or something, think again. This I can promise you."

"There's a chance you won't?"

"Let's say there was. So what? You're the vassal here. You're subservient to me. You can't change my mind. So nothing you do or say will have any bearing on what I do."

"But it's possible you won't incinerate me?"

"It's really damn small. I'd say less than 1 percent chance."

I thought of all the multiple versions of me that had split over and over and over again with all of the decisions of my life. Millions of them never reached the point where I was standing now. But millions of them had. There was an army standing behind me. And we would all probably be vanquished in a moment. But was it possible that there was one? Just one version of me that got to walk into our house and sit down with Sarah and tell her how sorry I was. That I would stop ignoring the ugly side of myself. That I would share everything with her. That we could still be the couple who climbed onto the roof together and watched the sky.

Any of the millions of me could be the one to make it past the dragon, to make ammends. We only needed one.

I wished that one me the best of all possible luck. Then I took a step forward.

**Part 4:
The End Is Nigh**

Tale #13: Rescue Mission

The men draw their swords, and the Harpy laughs
at their foolishness, as their swords are no good
against the natural elements she wields.

— Shakespeare, *The Tempest*

Felicia and I hadn't been getting along lately, but we both loved
our apartment. I'm pretty sure she would have broken up with
me at some point, but before we could discuss it, a significantly
disfigured harpy clutched her by the shoulders and yanked her
from the place where we split rent and utilities.

The harpy had crashed through the enormous bay window,
spraying shards of glass all over the IKEA furniture Felicia and
I bought a few months ago, after we ignored everyone else
in our lives and moved in together. The enormous bay window had been a major selling point, basically the only thing
we could agree on. It was kind of ironic that my last glimpse
of Felicia happened in the exact moment she was perfectly
framed in that window, her oval face a mask of confusion.

We'd known the apartment was near a harpy den, of
course. The landlord had to disclose it. But she assured us that
a harpy hadn't whisked away a human in what she described
as a very long time.

"Everyone is used to them," the landlord had said. "They're part of the town."

So, there I was, standing in the living room, a chilly wind blowing the hideous curtains Felicia's mom had given us when we moved in with Felicia now no longer here to defend them, and the first thought I had was whether she and I were still together.

Like, would she want me to rescue her?

Then my second thought was that maybe another harpy was coming, and I got out of there really fast.

Outside the apartment building, I found a bunch of people standing on the sidewalk looking up to the fifth floor at our enormous bay window as if the moment of Felicia's abduction was going to keep replaying like a highlight reel on the sports channel. Glass littered the sidewalk under their feet like confetti.

"That was awesome," a boy said. "I never believed harpies could do that. I thought they just ate fish out of the river and laughed at everyone's clothes."

There was a general murmur of agreement.

"Well, they do a lot more than that," I said, suddenly brimming with anger at these people enjoying what had happened to Felicia and our window. "That one took my girlfriend."

Everyone stopped talking and stared at me.

"Are you going to rescue her?" a man asked. "Because that's what the harpies expect. They aren't going to hurt her."

"What happens if no one rescues her?" I said.

"Don't you want to?" said a different man.

I looked to the boy who'd previously dubbed the whole situation awesome. "You want to do it?" I said.

"Go after your girl?"

I nodded.

"Hell no," he answered.

A woman pushed her way toward me and said, "Do you think you might move out now? How much is rent in this building?"

#

In truth, I pretty much liked everything about Felicia. The reason no one thought we were going to work was because my family and friends thought I didn't deserve her, and her family and friends thought I wasn't good enough for her. With that kind of pressure, it seemed like we were riding a self-fulfilling prophecy all the way to the final stop.

But the more we set out to prove everyone wrong, the more our differences became apparent. We spent so much time arguing over what couch to get and if the curtains her mom got us should go on the window or in the garbage, that we forgot how much we'd loved to be together. I could spend twenty-hours on a couch with Felicia, even if I hated the color, and watch movies and eat burnt popcorn and clutch hands as if one of us might float away. Or be snatched by a harpy.

Because there had been fire there, in our relationship. But buying furniture, decorating, paying bills, and deciding on every meal together had nearly doused it.

#

After I stormed away from the crowd in front of our building, I walked two blocks north and looked up at the harpy den. The harpies had taken over the twentieth floor of an office building many years ago. The twentieth-floor staff had gotten up from their desks on a hot afternoon to take part in a fire drill. As they assembled on the grass below, they watched a dozen harpies crash through the windows of their offices. Once the cruel creatures were huddled on the desks the workers had just abandoned, they began pointing down at the workers and laughing at their clothes and overall bad luck. And that's pretty much what they've been doing ever since.

Harpies wore strips of fabric and remnants of clothing they found in the trash, which they stitched together somehow with their claw-like fingers. These garments hung on them like multicolored rags, and they were intensely proud of their creations. Their unwashed hair hung in a similar manner over their mostly human faces. They also had thick brown wings that seemed incapable of flight but somehow weren't.

I'd never really seen a harpy up close before the one who had snatched Felicia right in front of me. I would sometimes see them flying in pairs to the river to catch fish, or sitting on top of the mall, where they laughed at the clothes purchases everyone made. But never as close as the one who'd taken Felicia. The one who was missing an eye. The one I would absolutely recognize if I saw her again.

The rest of the harpies' building was still in use by small insurance companies and IT departments. The den was a blight on the otherwise spotless building. It too was draped in extremely dirty multicolored tarps that covered the windows broken on that fateful day when they'd taken over the twentieth floor. What was it with harpies and defenestration?

I did not want to go up there. But, as far as I knew, that's where Felicia should be.

I cut across the parking lot, where mounds of harpy trash and droppings had rendered many parking spots unusable. The glass doors leading into the lobby didn't have a single fingerprint, so I tried to only touch the handle. When I entered, an older woman with a face that sagged on both sides gave me a smile.

"Welcome," she said. "How may I help you?"

"My girlfriend was taken by a harpy," I said with more panic than I expected in the totally silent lobby. A few people looked up from plush chairs where they were reading magazines.

The bland expression of kindness remained unchanged on the woman's face. "How unfortunate."

Her lack of concern made me question the rising agitation I was experiencing. There had to be an easy way to find out if Felicia was okay. "Is there anyone here who could run up and check on her real quick?"

"The only people who go up there are people launching rescue missions."

"Does that happen fairly frequently?"

"No. Never. Not while I've been here." She picked up a stack of paper and tapped the edges on the desk in front of her to line them up perfectly for no apparent reason, because the act of placing them back on the desk caused them to no longer be lined up. "But before I started working here, I heard of some rescue missions happening."

"How did it go? Was it easy?" I was really hoping it was easy.

"Some came back. But some didn't."

More than anything ever in my life, I didn't want to be a *some didn't*.

She sighed. "The elevator only goes to the eighteenth floor," she said. "The people who work on the floors above the twentieth arrive in helicopters each morning and take the elevator down to the twenty-second floor if needed."

"So how would I get up to the twentieth floor if, hypothetically, I wanted to?"

"I have no idea," the woman said. "Do you have an appointment?"

I left before I said something impolite.

#

When Felicia and I first started dating, I decided I wanted to work on my manners. I thought of her as this perfect thing, and I was the brute following her around. I didn't want her to be embarrassed of me when we went out with her friends or family.

I knew there was a better way to hold my fork and knife, and I was really interested in all the ways that I could be polite to her specifically. I began holding doors open and saying *please* and *thank you* and even *I'm sorry*. I once discovered a point of etiquette that she hadn't known previously, and that made me feel incredibly astute. It was this: If we were walking down a flight of stairs, manners dictated that I was supposed to go first.

"I'm not sure that's correct," she'd said.

"It's so that if you trip, I'll be right here to break your fall."

"Or catch me. You could catch me."

"My arms don't bend back that way," I'd said, and she laughed even though I hadn't meant it as a joke. That happened with us a lot.

#

Since the woman at the reception desk wasn't much help, I decided maybe I'd have better luck trying to get one of the helicopter pilots to take me to the top of the building. I wasn't planning to launch a rescue mission or anything. I just wanted to look in the den and make sure Felicia was all right.

It seemed like a fairly simple request for one of the pilots, considering the three of them were just standing around at the far end of the building's parking lot, laughing and smoking, their helicopters crouched on a hill behind them as if they might jump up at any moment. And once I'd checked on Felicia, I could go to the police station and fill out a harpy-kidnapping form and provide a detailed description of the harpy with one eye. Then I could get lunch and start cleaning up all that glass in the apartment.

"No," said the first pilot.

"No," said the second pilot.

"Yes," said the third pilot, "but only because I don't like being in agreement with these two assholes. Slight hiccup, though," he went on, turning to me. "I'm happy to take you, but, like, two minutes before you walked up, I lost my helicopter to these assholes in a card game."

"So you'll take me, but you don't have a helicopter?" I said.

"Precisely," the third pilot said and shook his head.

"Because of these assholes."

I looked up at the twentieth floor. It looked pretty quiet up there. I wondered, if our fates had been reversed, if Felicia would be trying this hard to check on me.

The second pilot, who up until this point had been scrutinizing me with a creased brow, narrowed his eyes until they were almost closed. "Are you on a rescue mission?"

I shook my head. "My girlfriend was taken by a harpy earlier, and I want to see if she's okay."

"Sounds like a rescue mission," he grumbled.

"Not exactly," I said. "I don't plan to fight or shout curses or sneak in while the harpies are sleeping. I want to make sure she's okay. That's it."

"But she was taken by harpies. Why would she be okay?"

That was a good question. "Well, I guess I want to see if it's preferable to being with me."

The three pilots laughed even though I hadn't meant it as a joke.

#

The helicopter ride was bumpy. The second pilot gave the impression that he wasn't the strongest of pilots. Before we took off, he kept twisting and turning some knobs on the dash and quickly scanning this dog-eared book in his lap. Once we were in the air, he pulled and pushed a lever between his knees, and we lurched up and up and up until we were on the roof.

"Sorry I can't maneuver past the windows. All I can do is go up and down. You can take it from here."

"I don't know how to take it from here," I said.

He grunted. "You have to get down to the twentieth floor."

"And then?"

"I don't know. It's your rescue mission."

"It's not a rescue mission. I think we might be about to break up."

"But you still love her?"

I very purposefully did not answer.

Then I got out and watched the helicopter shuffle to the edge of the building and basically tip off the side. I ran to the edge in time to see the pilot get the helicopter righted before he landed back near the parking lot with a thump.

A wind blew across the cement rooftop, and I suddenly felt very, very alone. And when I thought of everything beyond this rooftop, the rest of my life going forward from this moment, it seemed very lonely as well. I walked to the other side of the building and looked out at our apartment. I could just make out the large bay window, but I couldn't tell it was broken from here. Maybe from a distance, nothing ever looked broken.

I thought about Felicia's journey from that window to this building. It was probably over in a matter of minutes. She was ten floors below me now but had never felt further away. I knew if I walked through the large metal door leading into the building, there would be a stairwell, and I would walk down and I would keep walking down until I got to the twentieth floor.

And I would be on a rescue mission.

#

An hour or so later, a handful of workers emerged from the metal door. They looked at me quizzically as I remained cross-legged on the warm cement. I knew I couldn't sit there all day; I was starting to get sunburned. But I still wasn't ready to make any major life decisions.

One of the workers, a guy in a gray suit, went to the edge of the roof and began waving his arms around frantically. Another guy held up a large sign that said LUNCH in massive block letters and waved it in the direction of the pilots down below.

A woman in a long, flowery skirt approached me. "We're

about to go to lunch, but I couldn't help wondering. You work here? I've never seen you before." She cleared her throat. "This isn't a pickup line. Trying to figure out if I should call security."

"I'm stuck," I said. "My girlfriend was taken by a harpy earlier, and I don't know what to do."

"Okay, I'll call security."

"Wait," I said. "I haven't done anything!"

"Too late," she said and held out a little clicker about the size of a garage door opener that said SECURITY across the button that she was pressing over and over as she stared at me.

"You're right," I said. "It's too late."

I saw Felicia's face as she'd been whisked out the window. Could I have grabbed her? Was that her hand reaching out for me, or was I imagining it? Or could I have run into the elevator before the woman in the lobby stopped me, taken it to the eighteenth like she said, and walked up the rest of the flights? Or, instead of sitting on the roof and feeling sorry for myself and my predicament, I could have walked down to the twentieth floor already. Maybe when I arrived, Felicia's hand would have still been reaching out to me. What would it have felt like to grab her and pull her toward me? Now I would never know. Maybe I could at least plead my case to security.

There was a whoosh of air off the side of the building, and I expected to see the helicopter arriving to pick up the workers for lunch. But it was a harpy. More specifically, it was *the* harpy. The one from earlier. The one-eyed harpy. Her wings curved behind her like claws.

"This is the guy," the woman with the flowery skirt said as she ran off to join her group of co-workers. Even though this harpy was apparently the security for the building, she clearly still made the woman nervous.

The harpy landed with a thud on the roof and squinted her eye at me.

"I remember you from earlier," she said in a voice that didn't sound like it was used all that frequently.

"You took my girlfriend," I said.

She turned her only eye to me. "Girlfriend? I don't know about that. I think you two would have toughed it out a bit longer. Felicia likes the way you look for some reason. And you had some good times. But it wasn't a forever thing, and she wants a forever thing one day."

"She told you all that?" I said.

The harpy shook her head. "No, but she sees the wisdom in what her mother did. It's easier for both of you. Now you can skip that tough conversation. You can focus on your good memories. It's better this way."

My body was vibrating. "I'm sorry, are you telling me Felicia's mother hired you to do this?"

"Yes, of course. You think I just randomly wanted to grab a woman with questionable taste in curtains?"

"Exactly!" I said. "I hate those curtains."

The harpy took a step closer to me. "I think we're all surprised you are here, though. It's causing doubts down on the twentieth floor. Are you on a rescue mission?"

I'd been asked this all day. I'd never once given an honest answer.

The harpy's multicolored rags rippled in a breeze. Her wings shuddered slightly as if she was about to take off. It was hard being this close to her.

"I only want to make sure she's okay," I said.

"She's not with you anymore, so I'd say she's probably better."

"But did she say that?"

The harpy took a step toward me. "Why don't you ask her?"

And that's when I figured out that I wasn't scared of the rescue mission. I'd made it this far already. I was scared of what came *after* the rescue mission. Of Felicia's reaction.

The harpy took another step toward me. "I can take you to her. Fly you right down there. What do you say?"

Nothing would make a possible rescue mission easier than letting a harpy fly me directly to my destination.

The helicopter suddenly lurched up over the building in jerky, haphazard movements. Then there it was behind the harpy. And just as quickly as she'd grabbed Felicia earlier, the blades sliced off one of her wings.

The helicopter careened across the roof, sending the office workers scrambling before dipping down over the edge and disappearing from view.

The one-eyed harpy slumped to the ground with a groan. I knelt next to her, trying not to look at the bloody mess of her wing.

"What can I do?" I said. "How can I help you?"

"I need to get back to the den."

"I'll take you," I said without thinking first. "I'll help you get down there."

The harpy moaned in pain. She reached out to me, and I grabbed her gnarled, clawed fingers. Before I could help her to her feet, she pulled me roughly toward her.

"When we get to the stairs, I need you to walk in front of me." Her voice was like gravel in my ear. "In case I fall."

I looked her in the eyes. I could see how much pain she was in. Then I saw Felicia again. That same look in her eyes. She wasn't reaching for me. She was waving goodbye.

"She's not down there, is she?" I said.

"No," the harpy said weakly. "She left with her mother hours ago."

"She didn't expect me to rescue her."

"No."

I let that settle. Maybe our biggest problem was that we didn't expect anything of each other.

"Well, I'm on a rescue mission now," I said. "I'm going to get you back to your den. And I won't let you fall on the stairs."

"I suck at walking," she said.

"It's okay. That's one of the only things I'm really, really good at."

I helped her to her feet and she clutched my shoulders, the same way she'd grabbed Felicia's. Her breath was hot on my neck.

We reached the metal door, and I pulled it open.

"Don't let go," I said. "Don't let go."

Tale #14: Ache

How close to the moon does the tooth fairy soar
with her arms so full she can hold no more?
Could the tiny bright stars that hang in the sky
be the teeth that fell down as she flew by?

— Denise Barry,
What Does the Tooth Fairy Do With Our Teeth?

I fell in love at age seven. Twice.

The first time was with the exquisite pang I felt when I pushed my loose, upper-right lateral incisor with my tongue. I'd withhold that sweet ache from myself for hours, as if I was the drug dealer and my own best customer at the same time. I'd wait as long as I could, yearning for a fix, and finally another push and the engulfing ecstasy. I never wanted to lose that power. But the damn tooth ditched me while I was eating a peanut butter and jelly sandwich, and it didn't even have the courtesy to give me one last jolt. It wasn't until I crunched into it that I realized it had come out. I washed it off and stared at that pathetic deserter, angry that our time together had come to a close. Then I put it under my pillow that night, as I was told to do.

I then fell in love with the tooth fairy.

And my second love made me forget all about my first love. I no longer craved that perfect pain of a loose tooth. I only wanted to keep seeing her. Over and over and over again. And I knew, deep inside, that one day the tooth fairy would want to keep seeing me too. But there are only so many baby teeth a person can lose, and when the last one finally departed, my time with the tooth fairy came to a tragic close.

But I never got over her.

Claire knew of my infatuation, of course. In our tumultuous beginnings, I'd always tried to remain honest. She wasn't jealous. Not really. She didn't believe that I'd ever be successful in wooing a magical creature. She felt safe even though I told her that if I ever had the chance, I would take it. But we clung to each other. It was during our longest break-up that I decided to buy the ring, and then I thought we might try to make a non-magical life together.

"I'll make you forget her," she'd said that night as I extended the engagement ring.

"I guess you can try," I said.

She lowered her bright, trusting eyes to me. "If you bring her up again, I'll punch you directly in the face."

That seemed fair to me. She took the ring, so I figured we were all good. We jumped on that relationship escalator. We got married, separated for a time, bought a house, another short separation, and then we had a son who slowly grew a mouthful of teeth and got taller and started school and played sports and then, finally, after poking it with his tongue for a week, lost his first tooth.

I took a shower and changed into my favorite blue and pink striped shirt.

"Are you going to work?" my son said as I tucked him in after his bath.

"It's nighttime, buddy," I said.

"That's the shirt you wear to work."

"It's my lucky shirt," I said.

Claire snorted.

"Let's move on," I said. I turned to glare at Claire, and she shrugged her shoulders.

Claire had to understand that I wasn't going to miss seeing the tooth fairy. And I was so excited for her to see me all grown up. Other than being a lousy husband and father, I'd turned out pretty great.

"Where's your tooth?" I said to my son.

He looked really confused. "The one I lost?"

"Exactly."

"I don't know." My son yawned, exposing the place where his lower-right cuspid used to be.

"Come on, man. I told you to hang on to it."

"It's just a tooth, Dad."

"I told you it was important."

Claire clenched her jaw.

"It's probably on my desk or something," my son said.

"Go get it," I said.

"Can't I do it tomorrow?"

"No." I gave him my hardest look, eyes narrowed.

"Give him a break," Claire said. "He can look for it in the morning."

I glared at my son and talked in that quiet voice I used when I was angry. "You find that tooth and you put it under your pillow. Now."

"I really don't know what happened to it," he said, a small tear running down his cheek. "I had it on my dresser, but now it's gone." He looked to Claire, so I figured I'd leave and let them figure it out.

"When I get back, I want tooth under pillow? Got it?"

My son nodded at me.

"Don't you want a present?" I said.

"I guess." Another whimper.

"Of course you do. Now find the tooth, and I'll be right back."

There was no way I was wearing a work shirt when the

tooth fairy arrived, even if it was my favorite. I pushed past Claire without looking at her.

By the time she followed me into our bathroom, I'd already switched my shirt three times and stacked the discarded contenders on the sink.

"What's with all the shirts?" she said.

"I was figuring out which looked better."

"They all look good. It's the rest of you that could use some help."

"I'm not doing anything wrong. I just want to talk to her."

"In your best shirt."

"Maybe you're right. These shirts are too much. I need to tone it down." I moved across the room to the drawer where I kept all my T-shirts.

"I told him not to put his tooth under his pillow," Claire said.

"I figured," I said, even though I hadn't thought of that at all. I grabbed a maroon shirt because it would pop more in the glow from my son's nightlight.

"He's not going to find the tooth. So you can put the shirt away."

I turned toward her and really saw her for the first time since our son's tooth had fallen out. She looked hunched and defeated. In my excitement, I'd forgotten that Claire had feelings. And a lot of them had to do with me.

"I don't understand," I said. "I thought we had a deal."

"I thought we had a life together."

"We do. We always will."

"I know I've been distant lately," Claire said. "But from the moment that tooth started wriggling, I knew."

"Oh, Claire," I said. She looked so hurt. So vulnerable. I wanted to tell her that I would forget the whole thing. That what we had was more important. God, it would have felt good to do that.

"Let me just talk to her," is what actually came out. "Maybe nothing will come of it. And then that will be it."

"But that's just it. I don't want you to see what comes of it first. I want you to choose me. To forget all that past and focus on our future. Together. With our son."

"I have to know, Claire. Just give me the tooth. After this, everything will go back to normal."

Claire sighed. "It's a pattern with you. You push me away and then, just before I'm completely cut loose, you let me fall back into place. It's wearing me out. I can't hold on much longer."

I almost said it wasn't true, but I knew it was.

"What we have here, in this house, that's what is worth showing up for. Not some childhood infatuation. Plus, your son is upset. Really upset."

Then she punched me in my cheek, her knuckle smashing into my upper-right lateral incisor. I was impressed.

"I guess we had a deal," I said and rubbed my chin.

Claire shook her hand in front of her, her fingers slapping together. "God, that hurts."

"Well, my entire head is made of bone. There's hardly anything else there. Can I get you an ice pack?"

"Did you ever love me?" she asked.

I hesitated, even though the answer was yes. An unquestionable yes. Couldn't she see that I had? But she was gone before I opened my mouth.

Her absence felt final in the same way a tooth can never be reconnected to the gum. I'd always believed she'd never go away, no matter how hard I pushed. Now I could never tell her how she had made me forget about my first love, but I'd been too much of a fool to notice. I shut off the bathroom light and stepped into the hallway.

My son was sitting up in bed, eyes red from crying. Hair flattened from where Claire had been rubbing it. "I put the tooth under my pillow," he said as I sat at the foot of his bed. "Mom found it."

"Good boy. That's a good boy. Dad's not mad at you." I poked at my incisor with my tongue and felt a dull throb.

My son peered at me to see if I was telling the truth. "For real?"

"For real," I said.

"What's the tooth fairy like?" He asked, and then it all came back and I was in my childhood bedroom, jerking awake as a shape moved under my pillow.

"She takes your tooth," I said. "And she leaves you a present."

My son put his head on his pillow and smiled. "I can't wait to meet her."

"Go to sleep," I said and he closed his dewy eyes. "It's better if you're asleep."

I watched his eyeballs twist under his eyelids until they finally stilled. Then I pushed harder at my incisor, my jaw aching with the effort. The pain ballooned, radiating through my gums until it was impossible to feel where it had begun. I pushed again. I looked down at my maroon shirt, and a sliver of blood ran from my lip and splashed onto the front. I pushed harder. Again. And again.

I wasn't going to stop until the tooth was gone.

Tale #15: Blurry

The search for the monster has probably consumed more money, time, and newspaper space than attempts to prove the existence or otherwise of UFOs.

— Peter D. Jeans, *Seafaring Lore and Legend*

Jess and I were sitting on a faded gray beach, the same drab color as the sky, and when I looked out into the black water, the whole scene looked like a horizontal bar code. I was wearing the tiny red swim trunks she'd given me for my birthday a few years ago, even though I'd discovered this morning that they cut off circulation to my legs. But I didn't want to be in a fight with Jess and be fat at the same time, so I kept them on all through the breakfast with her parents and during our precipitous trek down the rocky path to this precise stretch of beach.

It wasn't exactly a fight. We weren't arguing or issuing ultimatums. There was just that shift that sometimes happens, more frequently these days, where I felt like she was looking past me, waiting for someone to arrive. This was kind of a metaphor, but it was literal too. Her eyes wouldn't meet mine.

"So what's special about this spot?" I asked, mostly because there were much easier places to reach. But she'd insisted it had to be here.

"I wanted to see if you'd follow me." She was wearing a new bikini top that resituated her breasts in a way that made them look brand new to me. Her choice of beachwear said very clearly that she was moving forward while I, sitting there in my red shorts, was stuck in the past.

"Do I get a prize?"

"Well. I did think it was going to be harder to get down here." But at least she smiled.

A wind pulsed from the sea, and the hair around my nipples stiffened. It had been a long time since I'd gone without a shirt, and I wasn't enjoying it at all. My arms were too skinny compared to the size of my newly-created paunch. "There's not much to see."

"That's the point. There's no distractions. We can concentrate on what is really happening."

"I don't know what you mean."

"Which is exactly why we're here."

"Are you breaking up with me?" I tried for it to sound like a joke.

She waited a long time. Long enough for me to regret saying it.

"I can always count on you," she said. "I know that."

It was strange how she was complimenting me, but it sounded like a slight. I was letting her down just by being me.

"Were you hoping I wouldn't follow you here?"

I suddenly wished I'd bought new swim trunks. Ones that I'd picked for myself that matched my altered body shape. Something that would let Jess know that I noticed things were changing too. And that I was capable of adapting.

A cold wind pulsed across the beach, slipping through the space between our shoulders.

"I was hoping he would show up," she said finally.

"Who?" I said, a little angrily, picturing a scene where I was confronted by some guy Jess was seeing on the side. And here I was in these fucking shorts.

"The Loch Ness Monster."

I sighed. Partly in relief, but also a bit of exasperation. It had become fashionable in the last few years to see the Loch Ness Monster all over the world, thousands of miles away from his home in Scotland. Though no one ever seemed to get a good picture.

"He was spotted down here," Jess said. "Rising in and out of the water. Gliding along the surface. Splashing his enormous tail. It seemed like something we should see."

"You think if anyone actually got close to it, like, close enough for a picture, that it would tear them limb from limb? That maybe we aren't supposed to see him? And if we do, there would be consequences?"

"I figured you wouldn't understand." She leaned back on her hands, her delicate fingers sinking into the sand, and fixed her gaze out into the void in front of us.

But I wanted to. I desperately wanted to understand the mystery of Jess. She was like my own private Loch Ness Monster, never fully in focus. We'd had some good times, but those were also getting lost in the fog.

"What if we see him today?" I said. "What do you think would happen?"

"That's the best part," Jess said. "We have no idea."

At that moment, I did the only thing I could. I looked out into the sea. The waves were ribbons of gray, roaring like a TV with no signal. I felt Jess next to me, warm and supple. There was a time when it would have been okay to put my arm around her waist and fall into her. But instead, I tried to figure out the exact point she was staring at, hoping that, in some small way, we could be in synch again.

Jess inhaled sharply a second before I saw it. An indistinguishable mass rising from the water. Its blurred edges made it hard to tell how far away it was. Or how big.

"Do you see him?" Jess whispered.

"I see *something*," I said, unable to convince myself that the

Loch Ness Monster was out there.

A sonorous bellow sounded from the murk, and then the shape began to move. It definitely moved.

"What's he doing?" I asked.

Jess turned to me and smiled. "He sees us."

Another bellow, and then the blurry shape doubled in size, was moving through the water toward us. I tried to focus my eyes, willing the creature to take shape in front of me, but it remained as elusive as any picture I'd ever seen of it.

"Maybe we should leave, Jess."

"Not yet."

She got slowly to her feet, and I watched the way she unfolded, the barest outline of her spine showing through her honey skin. I knew in that moment that if I couldn't pull her attention away from whatever was coming toward us, I'd never see her again.

The waves crashed with increased intensity as Jess stepped toward the water. The rounded back of the creature was visible now, along with the gentle curve of its neck. Or was it just a boat? Or a whale? Or an iceberg far from its home?

The sound came again, so close that my hair vibrated. I reached for Jess's hand, but she was too far away now, her towel whipping against her knees.

I didn't want to see Jess torn apart, a thread from her bikini the only evidence that she'd ever been here. And I certainly didn't want to see her carried away from me, her thin arms clutching the monster's neck as she was taken out to sea. I didn't want to see because I knew deep down inside that I couldn't follow her.

So I took a deep breath, hugged my legs to my chest, and closed my eyes.

Tale #16: Going Peacefully

An idea, like a ghost, must be spoken to a little before it will explain itself.

— Charles Dickens, *The Lamplighter*

While my wife got her hair cut, I went across the mall to a popular children's clothing store to choose an outfit for a newborn boy. Semantically, it was incorrect, though, because the boy wasn't actually newborn yet. He was currently unborn and residing in the abdomen of Maddie in the HR department of my office. Her husband was a lawyer, and there was no pressure for Maddie to work, something I could never hope to achieve for my wife.

My wife and I had agreed before we got married that we wouldn't have children. I went to a urologist a few months before the wedding, and he and I talked about our favorite restaurants in town while he breached my ball sack and snipped my vas deferens. My wife picked me up after the procedure, and with a bag of ice splayed across my lap, we tried one of the restaurants the urologist had suggested. Those were happy times, when what I looked forward to the most was the elimination of condoms from our sex life.

My mother would have been disappointed about our decision not to have children. But she was dead, and that made it much harder to be disappointed about things. She'd died while I was in college. I was twenty years old at the time, and I tried not to think about my mother at all. Her many attempts to meet someone new, someone to take care of her, sent her to trivia nights at bars and guided tours through American cities and lunches at museum cafeterias. She wanted to be loved, and she wanted to devote the entirety of her time and energy to someone other than herself.

My mother died alone in her bed on a cruise ship in a room with no window even though I'd encouraged her to upgrade. Passing from the pitch black of her room to the pitch black of the unknown without noticing the transition. Apparently, people died on cruise ships all the time. They have a department for it.

"Your mother went peacefully," a voice too young to know said to me over the phone from somewhere in the world I would never see. But the joke was on the cruise lines. My mother had never known a peaceful day in her life.

#

As I looked at brightly colored newborn outfits replete with repeating sequences of cartoon animals and extremely friendly-looking aliens, it was clear to me that my mother would have preferred for me to marry someone like Maddie. She wasn't beautiful or anything as simple as that. But she wasn't complex either. Maddie contained joy, and I had never been drawn to that. Now, though, Maddie's ability to look forward to the next day, to be excited to share that with others, including an unborn child whom she hefted around inside her body like a metaphor for her future, was supremely alluring to me. I felt compelled to bring a gift that would be the most cherished. One of which Maddie would be unable to stop thinking. Once her husband, Steven the Lawyer, had cooed quietly over the presents and then deleted them from his mind, he'd kiss Maddie on the head and leave the house to meet with a client. Maddie would linger in the new nursery whose paint color she'd asked for all our opinions on.

I could see her there as if I'd been invited.

The light from a football-shaped lamp illuminated the wall color I had chosen, just like in the picture she'd emailed the office after she and Steven the Lawyer had finished painting. She would pick up the outfit I'd purchased for her future son, and she'd rub it on her cheek to relish the softness. Then she'd catch a faint whiff. A droplet of my sweat. A trace of the cologne my wife had given me for our second anniversary—and Maddie would inhale a little harder. Trying to find it again. A brief sense of longing. Then she would hold the outfit in front of her to admire it. She'd picture her currently unborn son wearing it. Maybe even caress her swollen belly.

This image was very clear to me as I stood there in the popular children's clothing store. I could perfectly visualize the outfit she was holding, so that was the outfit I purchased. I put it in a plastic bag, hesitant to let my wife see it, and I returned to the salon to find that my wife had cut her hair to look like my mother.

#

Not long after we got married, my wife found an old album with my baby pictures. My mother and father appeared in many of them, though they were both dead now. Alcohol proved too much for my father to handle, and he was lucky he didn't take anyone out with him when his life came to an end on an unseasonably snowy road. His loss didn't register much at the time and didn't register at all once I reached adulthood. But in the pictures, my mother looked alive. It was hard to imagine that her timeline had come to an end.

My wife had lingered on her. Brushed her thumb across

my mother's cheek as my mother smiled at someone out of frame. "She's lovely," my wife had said. She'd picked her favorite picture and had it framed for me as a gift. But I didn't want a picture of my mother in our house. This framed photograph was, in fact, something my wife very much wanted, and she'd hung it at the end of the hall. The frame was stark white, and the picture was faded, but my mother's neediness was there, palpable in our house now.

I tried to brush against it a few times with my shoulder, hoping it would fall to the floor and break. An accident. But my mother's image clutched to the wall in the same way she'd clutched the belief that someone would make her happy one day. That someone would take on that burden for her.

"You have the haircut from that picture," I said as we lay in bed that night after the mall.

"Which picture?" my wife said, innocently.

"In the hall. My mother."

My wife brought her hands to both sides of her head, as if patting her hair allowed her to see it. "I didn't think of it that way, but I suppose it's similar. Could be passing it every day put it in my mind. Subconscious. Did you find a baby gift?"

"No," I said. "I just got a gift card."

Because we were both still awake for once, I asked if she wanted to have sex.

"Yes," she said without hesitation.

I turned off the light before commencing.

#

The newborn outfit was a beautiful, deep seafoam green. The shirt had a white collar that brought to mind sailors or Shirley Temple. Emblazoned on the front in a bold, puffy material was the image of a whale, the same color white as the collar. The whole shirt was the size of a paperback book. The trousers had legs about the length of my hand, and the seafoam green was only broken by a white tie around the waist.

Lying in bed, post-coital, my wife and I both content knowing that no child could be produced by our act, I pictured myself waking in the morning and opening my closet. There was the outfit, hanging among my button-up work shirts and my wife's muted blouses. But it was no longer sized for a newborn. I could tell as I stood there in my boxers, my wife still asleep in the bed with her mouth slightly open, that it would fit me perfectly. I brushed the back of my hand across the puffy whale, and it sent a thrill up my arm and into my neck. My body flushed. I buried my hands in the lush material and hoisted it from the closet.

I sat at the edge of the bed, careful not to wake my wife as the sun peeked over the horizon, and pulled the shirt over my head first. It whispered across my skin as it settled perfectly into place. The collar fluttered against my chin. I then pulled on the trousers and stood so I could confidently tie the drawstring around my waist. It was a glorious moment, a completion. I shivered with pride.

I looked over at my sleeping wife, her hair still visible in the pale light from the window. My mother's hair. I wonder if this was how they found my mother in her bed on that cruise all those years ago. Lying silently on her back, her hair settled on her pillow. Just as the young man from the death department had told me: She'd gone peacefully. But that wasn't exactly it though, was it? *Unknowing* would be more accurate. It wasn't peaceful. It was a surprise attack.

It was hard to look at my wife, lying there like that.

#

The baby shower happened at exactly 3 p.m. the next day. Everything happened exactly on time in our office. Maddie walked into the breakroom and smiled at everyone as if she hadn't expected to see us gathered there, even though she had been instrumental in arranging it.

She would never know that I didn't bring anything. It would mean nothing to her. She had no idea what my sweat or cologne smelled like. We had never spoken outside of email.

#

Another problem with my wife's haircut was that it was a perfect encapsulation of my mother from the time I was in elementary school. After my father had died. When I was out on the baseball field as a child, unable to tie my own shoes, which my mother attributed to grief over my father's death but I knew was just laziness, that was the haircut that left the bleachers and met me on the field. That was the haircut I looked down on as my mother's long fingers created two bows with laces on my cleats and pulled them tight. That was the haircut that filled me with shame. The haircut from the time when I was the sole receptacle for my mother's affections. Her attentiveness. Her involvement in every classroom activity.

Every morning, I wanted to get away from her. Every afternoon, I dreaded discovering her beyond the school doors, where no other parents waited. Alone and anxious, peering into the school to make sure I was still alive. That I was going to rejoin her. My mother's presence had begun to fill me with foreboding. I tortured her sometimes. Hiding in the bathroom until all the other students had left, my mother quivering at the bottom of the stairs, looking around, eyes wild. The haircut. The haircut. The haircut.

#

"I took a good look at the picture this morning," my wife said after work a few weeks after that fateful day at the mall, accosting me on the way to the shower. Her hair had grown out a little, which softened the memories it had exhumed.

"My hair doesn't look anything like your mother's. You're projecting."

"If it's not exact, it's exact-adjacent."

"Walk down the hall," she said. "Go down there and really look at it. Then try to explain to me why you're avoiding me."

My wife waited a moment to see if I was planning to do as she had commanded. When I didn't, she went into the bathroom and shut the door, and that ruined my plans to take a shower.

I went to our room instead. Our bed was unmade. After a year in this house, neither of us had taken up the mantle of bed-maker. Which suddenly seemed wrong. Why hadn't we discussed who was in charge of making the bed every morning? Why wasn't there a schedule?

I opened the closet as if I was going to find the newborn outfit there, waiting for me. A sense of hope and elation. But it was only my work shirts and my wife's blouses intermixed, huddled together for warmth. Some of the sleeves intertwined.

I returned to the bathroom and gently opened the door. My wife sat on the edge of the tub. The haircut suited her, of course. That's why she'd gotten it. It was bushy, the back slightly longer than the front, like she was going to join a hockey team. It framed her thin face perfectly.

"You look nice," I said and sat next to her.

She leaned forward, her elbow on her knee, and rested her chin on her upturned hand. I almost recoiled. That was the pose. It was exactly as my mother had looked the night my father died. The moment she transferred her unyielding need from him to me. The moment I began to matter too much. More than I ever wanted to.

I put my arm around my wife but averted my gaze from the mirror.

"Who was the first to say they didn't want to have children?" she asked.

"You." Of course it was her.

"I thought it was you."

"Have you changed your mind?"

"No," she said. Blunt.

"Me either."

My wife didn't move. Not one single muscle.

"So why are we upset?" I said.

She didn't answer me.

#

I never told my wife about the pregnant girlfriend in high school. It was solely for my mother to know, and of course, she would never know anything again. I was only fifteen when I had confessed, and my mother hadn't given me a lecture on using condoms or practicing abstinence or how I was too young to be a father. She was like a sun about to supernova.

"I'm going to smother that child," she said. "With love."

But all I had heard was "smother." And I believed her.

When the baby died before reaching the second trimester, my girlfriend blamed me for it. She said it was because I didn't want the child, that I already resented it. I had murdered our child with my indifference.

It was a crushing blow to my mother, who had never even met my girlfriend. Now she'd lost the grandchild and her future daughter-in-law.

But how could she not know? She must have known. That none of it was true. How could it be? I had no time away from my mother to meet a girl or consummate a relationship. My mother surely knew that. But she wanted to believe that story. Her belief was so strong that she let me create a child out of nothing. And then kill it.

#

After our conversation in the bathroom, my wife and I independently decided we would act as if everything was back to normal. We tried to remain in each other's eyesight when we could, instead of ducking into the nearest room and closing the door. We ate dinner together again. We kissed upon departure. What we hadn't done was appear together in public.

The night of her firm's office party, I told her I'd meet her there so I could have my own car. In case I needed to flee. I manufactured a reason to remain at work for an extra hour. I brought the outfit with me, tucked in my briefcase among document folders and legal-sized notebooks.

After everyone had left, I pulled it out and placed it on the desk. I ran my fingers around the edge as if I was making a chalk outline after a murder. I put my head down and pressed my cheek against the whale. I hoped that whatever power it contained would transfer to me so I could get through the next few hours of my wife's office party.

I drove across town and parked in the underground garage. I made sure my briefcase was locked, and I jammed it under the passenger seat so no one could see it. I was suddenly extremely nervous that someone would break into the car and take the briefcase, unaware that they would be acquiring the outfit too. I couldn't let the outfit get away from me.

After testing the view through multiple windows to see if the briefcase was visible and confirming that it was completely hidden, I decided to take the stairwell up the three floors to my wife's firm, rather than the elevator. And that's how I saw the touch.

My wife was talking to a woman, positioned in what I think was an attempt to watch the elevator. To look for me. The woman had her back to the elevator, and as I exited the stairwell, I watched her touch my wife on the elbow in a way that said she had touched that elbow before. And perhaps other places.

Before my wife noticed me, I immediately turned around and left.

#

I entered our empty house clutching my briefcase. Everything was dark and silent, as if everyone in the world had suddenly disappeared and I was the only person left. I moved toward our bedroom, careful not to look down the hall at the picture of my mother. I unlocked my briefcase and extracted the outfit. The moment I had it in my hands, I felt immediately better. At peace with my thoughts. Everything was mere curiosity now. Did that woman like the haircut? Had my wife cut it for her instead of me?

Before the thought had truly coalesced into an idea, I was unbuttoning my work shirt and tossing it to the ground. Then I undid my belt and let my trousers fall. I pulled off my boxers, my skin puckering on the parts of me that didn't get much time in the open. I pushed my briefcase off the bed, and my papers and notebooks splashed to the floor. I lay down gently on my back, the outfit clutched in my right hand. I took a few deep breaths, and then I placed the shirt on my chest. The material felt soft against my breastplate. I placed the small trousers just under my belly button, the soft mound of my belly rising above them.

I closed my eyes and pondered how much of me remained uncovered. The outfit barely shielded any of me from the world. I was pale and vulnerable, and everything that was available to see was lacking depth. I was a disappointing creature in a disappointing world with absolutely nothing that made me feel safe.

The door to the room opened then. A soft click. A whoosh of displaced air. I didn't open my eyes. It was easy to imagine my wife there, looking down at me. But it was also just as easy to picture my mother.

The door closed, and I was left alone again.

I got up. The outfit slipped off me and onto the unmade bed. With my eyes still closed, I began pulling at the tiny shirt.

Rearranging the molecules. Stretching it beyond what physics would allow. I pulled the shirt over my head, and it sunk down across my frame, covering my top half completely. Then I yanked the legs of the trousers, pliable now, willing them into the desired shape. I stood and put one leg in at a time inside. The fabric brushed against my thighs as I pulled the drawstring tight. I felt the weight of the whale on my chest. I finally opened my eyes, but I didn't look down. I didn't want anything to ruin this moment.

I slipped out of the room and saw a sliver of light coming from under the bathroom door. My wife wasn't ready to see me like this. Instead, I looked down the hall. My mother's framed picture barely visible in the twilight.

I moved slowly toward the picture, my mother's face materializing out of the gloom. The haircut, of course, was just as my wife had said. Barely a passing resemblance.

Something clanked in the bathroom behind me. My wife grunted. Then the unmistakable sound of hair clippers connecting with scalp. I wanted to turn back, to stop her. But I was close enough now to the picture, closer than I'd been in a long time, and I noticed something I'd never seen before. Down at the bottom of the frame. It was me. A tiny baby. Not knowing what lay ahead for me. Most of me was cut off, lost forever in a past never to be recovered. I leaned closer, and my breath sent the frame tumbling to the floor. The light from the bathroom illuminated the picture, that nascent image of me. But it was clearer now. I no longer seemed unaware. Down there, hovering at the bottom of the frame, I could see a look of sheer terror on my face amid the faintest hint of seafoam green.

Tale #17: Loss

"What is a chupacabra?" asked Merrilegs, sounding alarmed. "It's a mysterious Animal that can't be caught. A vengeful Beast."

— Olga Tokarczuk,
Drive Your Plow Over the Bones of the Dead

Every night, my daughter spent the minutes before bed diligently writing in the notebook she'd bought at her school book fair. The notebook had the words MY MOM IS MY SUPERHERO scrolled across the front in a font so indecipherable that I finally had to break down and ask my wife what it said.

"It says I'm her hero," Daphne said.

I nodded assent. "They must have been out of the ones that said MY DAD IS A FAILURE."

"Yes, I suppose they were," my wife said. "A lot of failing dads out there. High demand amongst their offspring to advertise it."

It made me sad to think about the secret divorce paperwork that I hadn't given her yet.

Daphne used to be really into me, but now I knew she found me super aggravating. She just hadn't admitted it yet. One day I called her mom while Daphne was out running to see if she had any advice for me on how to proceed with her daughter.

"If you're coming to me," Daphne's mom said, "then it's too late." That's when I knew it was over between Daphne and me.

A few days later, Daphne started leaving a bowl of uncooked red meat on the back patio.

"What's with the meat?" I said.

"We have a cat now," she said. "But it doesn't seem to like milk or dry food or anything. It decimated some expired meat I had in the bin, though. So now I just hook it up."

"You're the stray cat's dealer?"

"Yes," she said but didn't laugh because when you're bored of someone, that person ceases to be funny.

#

The story my daughter was writing every night was about a Chupacabra. At the beginning, it is skinny and tired and very very hungry. "Like that caterpillar in the story you read to me when I was a kid," she explained. She loved to talk about when she was a kid even though she was only eleven.

In thickly verbose prose, my daughter described the squalid conditions of the Chupacabra's hillside home, its propensity for violence toward the small rodents also living in squalor, and the way its ribs poked through its skin like tent poles. But even with all that precise description, I still had no idea what a Chupacabra looked like.

After a few weeks without finding a single shivering rodent to massacre, the Chupacabra decides to leave the home he had always known with the hope of finding a better life. The journey teems with the Chupacabra's interiority and his struggle with existence and morality and the question of whether there was a meaning to be discovered in it all.

"Are you reading my story?" my daughter asked from her bed, where I thought she'd been asleep for the last few hours.

I was holding my phone light over the pages of the notebook, my face only a few inches from my daughter's tiny scrawl. I had to admit I was reading it, but I wouldn't tell her how many times I had read it previously.

"It's riveting," I said.

"Wait until you see what happens tomorrow," she said and then rolled away from me. I put the notebook on her desk and then kissed her on the head. She still smelled exactly as she did as a baby. Slightly earthen. Or like a smooth rock left in direct sunlight day after day.

I shut her door softly and went into the kitchen to find something to eat. Ever since Daphne and I had been on the outs, I had lost nearly fifteen pounds due to an overarching sadness and not eating family meals together. I knew that once I served the paperwork and we officially split, I wouldn't see my daughter every day anymore. I wondered how long until my ribs would look like tent poles.

I opened the refrigerator, and the light spilled over the back door, which caused something heavy and rasping to bang against it. The glass panes rattled. All the hair on my arms rose to meet my shirtsleeves. A horrible snorting sound barreled across our backyard.

With some reservation, I moved to the window and tried to catch sight of whatever it was. Next to the small shed where I kept our lawnmower, two unblinking yellow eyes stared back at me. My mouth went dry.

Suddenly Daphne was next to me opening the back door.

"Don't open that!" I managed to yell.

She ignored me, of course, and leaned down to retrieve an empty bowl.

"Cat was hungry tonight," she said.

I looked out the window again, but the eyes were gone.

#

The next night, the Chupacabra finds a farmhouse. The field

around it is literally crawling with goats. With chilling depictions of severed arteries, torn flesh, and an atheistic belief in only itself, the Chupacabra eats every last one of them.

I looked at my daughter asleep in her bed and felt this deep, unfathomable loss. She was growing and changing and adapting, and somehow I had stayed exactly the same. She no longer needed me. That much was clear. I had devoted my time, all of it, my everything. And every day, she needed less of it. She needed less of me. This simple subtraction, like the math problems I used to help her with, was easy to calculate. The numbers kept going down until they reached zero.

Once, not so many years ago, she and I had spent an afternoon arguing whether zero was a number. She said it wasn't. That it was an absence of numbers. But I believed it was a number. I always had. It was a starting point. It was an ending. It was there to remind you of where you were and where you still had to go. Without zero, there was no place to stand between all the failures and the occasional wins. Zero had to be solid, a firm spot to place both of your feet.

But now, in the dim light of her room, the sound of her soft breath like the most placid of oceans, I wasn't so sure. Had I been wrong all along? By choosing to believe that zero was a solid landing point, had I guaranteed my own erasure? Had I written myself out of my daughter's future?

I thought about that Chupacabra at the farmhouse, ripping those goats to shreds. He was my fucking hero.

#

When Daphne and I met, I had what they called a bright future ahead of me. I'd just gotten a role in a recurring series of commercials for a mobile phone network. The first commercial featured me and this other guy sitting in a cafe. He had perfect service because he used the mobile phone network we were selling, and I kept walking around the cafe with my phone aloft, trying to get reception. Over the course of thir-ty-four seconds, I managed to spill my coffee on my laptop and ruin my big work presentation, and then, while standing on a chair, I set off the sprinkler system. Then I stepped onto a crowded table that riotously broke and sent an array of knives whizzing by my head. With pinwheeling arms, I knocked over not one, not two, but ten cups of coffee in rapid succession and then somehow sent a motorized wheelchair zooming into a busy intersection. I was an immediate hit and became a household name, or at least face, for a very short time.

During that very short time, Daphne and I got married.

She wanted to be with someone with goals. Someone with a plan to turn a lucky role in a commercial into a career. Maybe someone who she could go to the Oscars with someday.

Then I quit acting.

The thing is, Daphne was a huge success. She got an MBA and was now running the HR department for a massive com-pany that I didn't really know anything about what they did other than pay Daphne a lot of money. I worked here and there, and I even got an online computer programming cer-tificate. But once our daughter arrived, it was assumed that I would be the primary caretaker.

It turned out to be my best role. I changed her diapers, made sure she ate, and rocked her to sleep. I helped her with her homework and picked out all her clothes. I brushed her teeth and took her to the dentist and the doctor and gave her any medication she needed. Until recently, she and I had eaten every dinner together. I was adrift while she was at school, counting the hours until she returned.

But the more my daughter became self-sufficient, the more Daphne and I grew apart. Essentially, I was useless. I was the moderately attractive guy from those commercials you kind of remember who was now balding and had a tightly swollen belly with patches of hair where patches of hair shouldn't be. I wasn't needed here anymore. But if I left, I'd be losing the only place that had ever had a true place for me.

#

Daphne was in the kitchen, slapping wet, raw meat into the bowl.

"I can help you with that, if you'd like," I said. For a second, I could see the future where I parlayed my years of childcare into animal rescue and thereby secured a new spot in our home.

"I can manage."

"You know it's not a cat, right?" I said.

"It needs me," she said. "Doesn't matter what it is."

The muscles on her arms were taut strings that I longed to caress. "I feel like I have to ask permission to touch you."

She finished with the raw meat and began washing her hands vigorously in the sink.

I moved toward her.

"Don't," she said.

I stopped and continued watching her. Then I laughed. "You know what word I just thought of?"

"I couldn't possibly." Still washing her hands.

"Caress. I don't think I've ever used that word before. Or thought of it. It's not that I wanted to touch you. That's not it, exactly. Caress is different. It's softer. It's touching with meaning. I wanted to send you a message with my hands."

"That's the nicest thing you've ever said to me." I could see she was crying.

"It's true." My hands were aching for her to allow me this one request.

She opened the door and put the bowl of meat on the porch. She made a little whistle sound to call whatever monstrosity was out there. Then she shut the door and turned to face me.

"I know it's true. That's why I'm crying" she said, and then quietly left the room.

It would be a million times easier if she divorced me.

I shut off the light and stared into our yard. I knew whatever creature was out there was staring back at me. I could feel it. I felt a sudden warmth toward it. I wanted it to know that I could help it too.

I opened the door and nudged the bowl with my foot. The smell of it caused a wave of bile to begin exploring the back of my throat. Then the eyes appeared. Exactly where they had been yesterday. Piercing and yellow, and I guess I just have to say it: malevolent. I sent a mental apology out into the yard. I was still committed to befriending it.

Then the eyes shifted, and it took me a moment to realize it was coming toward me. Wheezing and rasping. Its feet swishing through the grass that was overdue for a mowing. It was still staring as it ran. It wasn't coming for the food.

It was coming for me.

I slammed the door as its claws scratched onto the porch. I jumped backward into the kitchen. It breathed loudly on the other side of the door. Huffing and puffing. Snorting. My heart beat so fast that I had to clutch the counter to remain standing. We were both waiting now. I couldn't move.

Then it began slurping up the meat, the bowl scraping across the cement like a body.

#

After school the next day, I asked my daughter if she wanted to go out for ice cream. She looked at me sadly, as if I had disappointed her with how lame I was, but after some reflection, she agreed to go.

We went to the place we had gone many times while Daphne was at work and both ordered our favorites without thinking. We didn't even look in the display. I love that kind of routine. When something is simple and easy. I wanted more of that in my life.

My daughter got chocolate brownie, and I got strawberry.

"I'm glad you came out with me," I said.

"I love ice cream," she said. "I wasn't sure if I was ready for the conversation yet. But I guess I am. Lay it on me."

"What do you mean?"

"Where you tell me that you and Mom are getting divorced. Or separated. And then I have to choose a side, I guess. And I know you'll never take me from mom."

"Your mom and I aren't getting a divorce," I said. And even with the paperwork in my sock drawer, I believed it. It wasn't the outcome I wanted.

"Then what's going on with you guys?"

"I'm a disappointment."

She looked really confused. "In what way?"

"I don't have a sweet career. I'm not bringing home the bacon, as they say."

"But you're the best dad ever. Mom knows that."

I looked at my daughter's face. She was an absolute marvel that I felt was impossible I had anything to do with.

#

That night, the Chupacabra story made a tonal shift, verging almost into screwball comedy.

Knowing that it has depleted its entire food source in one night, he knows he needs a desperate plan to get more. Because at this point in the story, he has decided to remain on the farm forever. The one human, a farmer of extremely advanced age, suffered a fatal heart attack when he beheld the Chupacabra ripping his goats to shreds. The Chupacabra now has a beautiful acreage of land, a solid roof over his head, and a firm mattress for sleeping. There is also a brief aside on how good the farmer tasted.

Then he takes the farmer's clothes and puts them on. He begins practicing walking around on two legs. He begins reading the *Reader's Digest* magazines littered around the farmhouse and listening to Frank Sinatra albums. Soon the Chupacabra is a passable man, and he saunters into town to strike a deal for more goats.

My daughter was pretending to sleep, I could tell. I wanted to ask her if she'd changed the story because of me. Because of our conversation earlier. Was she trying to tell me something? That I could become the man I wanted to be?

I called her name in the dark, but she didn't respond.

I got to the kitchen before Daphne arrived and decided to fill the bowl myself. The meat glistened in the refrigerator light. I cut open the packages and let the meat slither from the blood-soaked trays and into the bowl. When I was done, I checked the yard and the porch to make sure the creature wasn't waiting for me. Then I quickly opened the door and tossed the bowl out. I took a deep breath. Then I moved away, leaned against the counter, and waited. And waited.

But neither the beast nor Daphne showed up.

#

Now that the Chupacabra can pass as a man, he needs to find some new goats. In the farmhouse he has now fully taken over, he finds a trove of antiques the farmer's family had been hoarding for generations. The Chupacabra brings the antiques to a local merchant, and using the piles of money he made, he arranges for a local driver to bring a steady stream of goats to the farmhouse weekly.

It's a perfect plan that is only ruined when the Chupacabra has to kill the delivery guy, which then, of course, brings the attention of the entire village onto the farmhouse. Here's how it goes down: The delivery guy was just curious about where all the goats went each week. So late one night, after he and a friend have been drinking, they drive out to the farmhouse and park behind a small group of trees before sneaking to the farmhouse on foot. They see the farmer pull off his clothes, and—with still no clear description of what the Chupacabra looks like—they watch in horror as it eats its way through the goats. Repulsed, the delivery guy's friend makes a big scene and runs for the truck even though the delivery guy is frantically trying to calm him down. But the Chupacabra already saw them, and he easily catches the delivery guy while the friend drives away.

Within an hour, the entire village is outside the farmhouse with pitchforks and torches "like in some black-and-white movie" (the exact phrase my daughter used to describe the scene). The Chupacabra huddles in the farmhouse but knows he will be dead soon. And in that moment, he begins to fear death. Until now, it has never felt like something that could happen to him. He suddenly fears a world in which he would no longer be a part. He becomes frantic to stay alive as the mob descends.

And that's where it stops.

#

"Yes," my daughter said. "There's no more. That was the end."

"I can get you another notebook," I said.

"No, Dad. The story is over. I'm finished."

It was hard to know why I had such strong feelings for the Chupacabra. I thought this whole time he'd been the villain. That I should want him to fail. But now I'd rather the weekly goat delivery thing had worked out. The Chupacabra wasn't evil. He was just doing what Chupacabras do. And when he tried to change, to become a man, it got him killed.

"Can I keep this?" I said.

"Yes, of course, Dad. I wrote it for you."

I kissed her head, turned off the light, and left the room. The notebook suddenly felt heavier than ever before.

In the kitchen, Daphne stared out the window. "Cat's gone."

"I'm sorry," I said. "I tried to feed him last night, and he didn't show up either."

"I wonder if that's why?"

"You mean he left because I tried to feed him?"

"I don't know. Maybe."

I joined her at the window. "You know why I quit acting, right?"

She continued staring out the window, as if trying to manifest the monster she'd been feeding.

"I felt like a failure in life up until that point. And then my big role was a guy who was a failure. I could see the future in front of me. Honing the role of failure. Playing him on and off the screen. Then you came along, Daphne. And it was the only time I felt successful. So the acting didn't seem important anymore. Then we had our daughter, and I answered my true calling. I'm not a failure because I stopped acting. I'm a success because of it."

Daphne turned to me. "The problem isn't that I think you're a failure. It's that you think you're a failure."

We were closer than we'd been in months. I could feel her breath on my neck.

"I have divorce paperwork," I said.

"I know you do," she said.

Then she brushed past me, and I felt the true loss of her.

I looked out into the empty yard. Maybe I could find the creature, bring him home. Reclaim my place. I opened the door and moved into the grass. I would definitely cut it this weekend. When I reached the shed, I stopped and turned around. There was our small house that contained our past and whatever remained of our future. I'd left the light on in the kitchen.

Then I heard it. The raspy breath somewhere not too far behind me. I should have taken the bowl with me, something to distract it. I couldn't turn around. I felt the creature sidle up next to me. Its ragged breath hot on my legs. I waited for the feel of its teeth. For its claws to eviscerate me.

Instead, I felt its coarse flesh brush gently against my leg.

Part 5:
The End

Tale #18: The End

And how should we behave during this Apocalypse? We should be unusually kind to one another, certainly. But we should also stop being so serious. Jokes help a lot.

— Kurt Vonnegut, *Armageddon in Retrospect*

Miranda and I had a doozy of a fight last night, like the kind where we both started digging into the past for evidence to bolster our current charges. Then, by the time I woke this morning, the world had ended.

Neither of us had backed down, so we slept in the same bed, turned away from each other like question marks. I badly wanted to fall asleep first so she could see how unharmed I was by the fray, but she was snoring well before I drifted off. I thought about when we'd met and how, once I'd seen her, I never wanted to let her out of my sight. When we moved in together, she'd started calling me Duckling because I followed her from room to room, a few steps behind, a look of awe on my face.

This morning, I roll over with the intention of apologizing. I meant everything I said about feeling displaced and unsettled in our current life, but none of it is enough for me to end anything. This is the hazard of a relationship; I have to decide if I am losing myself or becoming better.

But Miranda is gone. And so is half of our apartment. As in, the wall along the east side of the building has been ripped free, taking with it my television and video games, which were the only things I brought with me when I moved in. The toilet was also along that wall, and in the kitchen, this means the loss of the refrigerator, the microwave, and the hanging pots we never used.

The sun slants across my face, and I raise my hand to block it. Through my fingers, I see that the building across the street has suffered a similar fate to ours. I can see into every bedroom. Each is empty of life. Everyone is gone.

I search our apartment, careful not to get too close to the edge, but there is no sign of Miranda. Wind gusts in and rifles loose papers, picture frames, and the books we will never read. I hope, somehow, that Miranda left in the night and that she is safe somewhere. But the chain is still on the door, and the only other way out would be through the missing wall.

I look down sixteen stories to the street below, and nothing is moving. There is no sound.

I eat dry cereal alone at the table.

I go out searching. I don't run into a single person. Nor any bodies. Every building, every car, every possible container of people has been ripped in half. The innards of everything exposed like gruesome autopsies. As if some creature cracked everything to suck out the inhabitants.

But I refuse to think of everyone as dead, only moved. Miranda didn't do well with change, though. She never got used to me sharing a space with her. Wherever she is now, whatever her new world looks like, I hope that everything is intact. That the insides aren't showing.

As for this world, I guess it can't officially be over unless there is someone here to see it.

Someone like me.

Acknowledgments

"Keening" originally appeared in Lunch Ticket

"Bingo" originally appeared in Okay Donkey

"Infinite Possibilities Outside the Screen" originally appeared in Short Story, Long

"Where the Magic Is" originally appeared in Catapult

"Therapy" and "Rescue Mission" originally appeared in Pithead Chapel

"The Lie" originally appeared in an altered form in BULL as "One-Time Offer"

"Classified" and "Waves" originally appeared in Vol. 1 Brooklyn

"Luck" originally appeared in wigleaf

"Court of Common Pleas" originally appeared in Terrazzo Editions and also in an altered form in Bending Genres as "Ash"

"Ache" originally appeared in X-R-A-Y

"Blurry" originally appeared in apt

"Going Peacefully" originally appeared in Split Lip

"Loss" originally appeared in The Rumpus

"The End" originally appeared in Hobart

Thank You

This is my third book and my third chance to write an earnest thank you to the people in my life who make this possible. With so many things vying for time and attention (not to mention overall exhaustion), it's easy to second-guess a project. Will this be worth all the effort? Will I wish that I had focused on something else instead? It would be impossible to find myself here with a completed *Magic Can't Save Us* without the support and encouragement I received along the way.

I wrote the first story in what would become this collection in 2017. Scott Garson at wigleaf published it, and he saw something in it that I hadn't seen yet. He recommended I read Arthur Bradford, who writes tonally-linked stories in a way that resonated with me, and he suggested that there was a life beyond just this one story in wigleaf. Not every story I wrote made it into the collection, but this one, entitled "Luck," I always knew would be in the final version. Thank you, Scott, for providing that spark.

I began writing more stories with this evolving theme. In 2019, as I started sequencing the stories in my very first collection, *Not Everyone Is Special*, with the absolutely life-changing 7.13 Books, run by Leland Cheuk, I was so excited about these nascent creature stories that I began shoehorning them in with the original stories. I want to thank Leland Cheuk, in perpetuity, for rekindling my desire to write when he accepted that collection for publication, and for being so incredibly kind and patient with me as I realized that these magical creature stories could one day be their own thing. Which, I must admit, prompted me to remove them from the final manuscript not far from publication. You are the best, Leland!

Some wonderful editors came along and began publishing these stories on their wonderful sites and in their wonderful journals. Working with these editors changed the way I looked at the stories and how I went about crafting them. In particular, I'd like to thank Karissa Chen, Eric Newman, Katie Quach, Gina Nutt,

Nicole Chung, Key K. Bird, Aaron Burch, and Kim Magowan.

A number of friends have read various versions of *Magic Can't Save Us* over the years. A special shout-out to Mark Jednaszewski, who not only read multiple versions but was always available to run ideas in an Instagram chat while he was out at sea. And I absolutely must thank as well: Amy Stuber, Alice Kaltman, Kurt Baumeister, Pam Susemiehl, Jennifer Fliss, K. C. Mead-Brewer, and Tyler Dempsey.

As a writer struggling in the writer world, it's nice to happen upon people who offer support and guidance and overall just send good vibes my way. Without that, it's too easy to think about giving up. For just being the people they are, I'd like to thank: Kimberly King Parsons, Carol Mitchell, Matt Bell, Amber Sparks, Sarah High, Tod Goldberg, Matt Salesses, Ben Loory, Tim O'Connell, Mark Haber, Cassie Mannes Murray, Adam Newton, Peg Alford Pursell, David Queen, Kevin Sampsell, Owen Egerton, Anna Vangala Jones, and Reneé Zuckerbrot.

I can't forget my Bookshop.org crew, who gets excited about my books even though we talk about hundreds of other books every single day. Thanks to Andy Hunter, David Rose, Katie Fleming, Angela Januzzi, Jill Meyers, Desi Tomaselli, and Daniel Berkowitz. A gigantic thank you to Steph Opitz for always having my back and for being available to hear any crazy idea I might have. Steph is such a positive force in the world of books, I feel lucky to know her. Another gigantic thank you to Rob Bieselin for also listening to my crazy ideas but then still deciding to make some lovely assets to use while promoting my books. And one more gigantic thank you to Amanda Rivera for reading this collection before nearly everyone else and then sending me screenshots of typos and for overall making me feel I'd written a book that people might enjoy!

A special thank you to Lori Hettler, a true champion of indie literature and an overall great person to have in your corner when you attempt to bring a book into the world. This is the second time Lori has helped me with publicity, and it's hard to imagine this agonizing experience without her cheering me on! And also thanks to Jeremy Wang-Iverson, who has a way of making publicity sound like a chill experience and has years of knowledge that he has allowed me to tap into. I learned a lot from Jeremy about being a marketer of my books, and I appreciate the help he has given me in getting the word out.

Publishing a book can be a stressful experience, for me most notably because that means it's time to ask other writers I admire if they'll read my book early (probably still riddled with typos) and provide a blurb. The writers I asked this time around are some of my absolute favorites, and I encourage you to seek out their books if you haven't already. You won't be disappointed. A forever thank you is herein supplied to Sequoia Nagamatsu, Fernando A. Flores, Ursula Villarreal-Moura, Amber Sparks, and Ben Tanzer. And yes, I have thanked Amber Sparks twice in these acknowledgments, and it was on purpose because she is so supportive and so kind and I'm grateful to have her on my side!

What can I say about UNO Press? What a lovely experience! I can still remember the feeling when Abram Himelstein emailed me to say they had chosen *Magic Can't Save Us* as the winner of the Publishing Lab Prize. I can remember that first Zoom meeting with Abram and G. K. Darby and the students in the program and how I could feel the excitement they had for my book. It was exhilarating. I did not want to let them down! But nothing compares with getting to work with Chelsey Kimberly Shannon. I have been lucky to work with some wonderful editors, but I have never had an experience like this, where, through the notes I received from Chelsey and the students in the program, I not only grew as a writer but as a person. We pushed and stretched and sometimes beat these stories into new shapes with greater insights into the characters and a deeper understanding of what it means to be human. Thank you so much, Chelsey, for working with me over a very eventful year. This book is so much better than it ever could have been if I had done it on my own. Truly, thank you for this experience, Abram, G. K., Chelsey, Alexa Torres,

Liv Demac, and all the students in the UNO publishing program. And thank you to Kevin Stone, from the bottom of my heart, for the most wonderful book cover I could have ever hoped for.

And finally, I find myself ready to thank the people who not only support me as a writer but who also comprise everything about me and every aspect of my life. To my three boys, Elijah, Ezra, and Moses, thank you for being curious and kind-hearted and funny and compassionate. And also for making fun of me mercilessly and for being so thoroughly impressed that you can search my name on the Internet. You make me a better person every day. And I hope one day, you will find it inspiring to learn how hard it is to get a book published! I promise there's one coming up soon that you can actually read! Thank you to Ah for putting up with all of us and for looking after us and for being the emotional core of the family. We wouldn't be pursuing any of our creative endeavors without you!

And now, Rebecca's favorite part of any of my books. The part where I say something potentially embarrassing but definitely so earnest that it sends her into spasms of laughter. Rebecca, it's true you have always supported me in so many ways, but you have always enjoyed the stories in *Magic Can't Save Us* more than any of my other projects. Knowing how much you loved them kept me going all these years. One day, I wanted to publish this collection and be able to tell you the proper way (in the back of the book in the acknowledgements, of course) that it wouldn't exist without you. It *couldn't* exist without you. If I know a story makes you laugh, it's the most successful I will ever feel in my life. You mean so much to me. Our life together with our boys is so incredible that everything else is secondary. The struggles and successes come and go, but having you with me makes me feel like I can do anything. I dedicate this book to you. Thank you for sharing everything in this life with me. As the world's greatest love poet once said: "You are the epicenter of hotness." I can't wait to see what comes next.

Permissions

Biography

Josh Denslow is also the author of *Not Everyone Is Special* (7.13 Books) and *Super Normal* (Stillhouse Press). His most recent short stories have appeared in Electric Literature's The Commuter, The Rumpus, and Okay Donkey, among others. He is the email marketing manager for Bookshop.org, and he has read and edited for SmokeLong Quarterly for over a decade. He currently lives in Barcelona with his family.